A
DECENT
WORLD

A
DECENT
WORLD

Ellen Hawley

Swift

SWIFT PRESS

This paperback edition published by Swift Press 2024
First published in Great Britain by Swift Press 2023

1 3 5 7 9 10 8 6 4 2

Text designed and set in Minion by Tetragon, London
Printed and bound in Great Britain by CPI Group (UK) Ltd, Croydon, CR0 4YY

A CIP catalogue record for this book is available from the British Library

ISBN: 978-1-80075-150-7
eISBN: 978-1-80075-149-1

For Ida

Easier to imagine the end of the world than it is to imagine the end of capitalism.

Origin uncertain.
Quoted by Frederic Jameson

All that is solid melts into air.

Karl Marx

T OWARD the end of the first real conversation we ever had, David Freund asked if I still thought I could change the world.

"Still," he said, as if we'd been arguing about this for years, although before Josie – my grandmother, his sister – died we'd never seen each other. She'd been the stopper in the family bottle, keeping him neatly contained and out of our lives, and now that she was gone, he was pouring into my life. Already he thought he knew what was inside my head. Which pissed me off, particularly since he was right.

I'd seen him twice since Josie's death and we hadn't managed much in the way of conversation either time. Here I was, though, sitting stiffly on his brocade sofa, trying not to spill the coffee he'd given me.

I quoted Margaret Meade at him: "Never doubt that a small group of thoughtful, committed citizens can change the world. Indeed, it is the only thing that ever has."

It felt odd saying "indeed" out loud, but the quote demanded that kind of formality. Besides, it matched his furniture.

He blew a stream of air through his lips as if it was exactly the sort of answer he'd expected. I told myself I was a stand-in for the version of Josie he carried in his memory, and the whole scene seemed as natural as it did ridiculous.

I'd borrowed my quotation from a battered poster still taped to Josie's basement door, so in a sense it was her answer.

1

As a kid, I read the words so often that I'd stored them on the mental shelf where our most fundamental beliefs share space with our platitudes: Safety is fragile; if we drop things, they fall; a small, committed group of people can build a just society.

Long after I left David's house, our answer, Josie's and mine, bounced around in my head.

Did I still agree with it?

Mostly.

Partly.

Entirely. I couldn't face a life where I didn't. But it was easier to believe if we were talking about the small things. I'd started to wonder about the big ones.

Josie never did. The Soviet version of socialism had shaped her life, but even after the Soviet Union collapsed, she held steady. A small group of committed citizens, et cetera.

I don't remember the collapse. My entire experience of Josie – not to mention of the world – dates from the post-Soviet era, with capitalism triumphant and crumbling and our lovely, spoiled planet floating like a lobster in a pot of warming water while we, the complicated little parasites who live on its back, tell each other we're still okay.

Believing we can change the world has never been easy, and it's at least as hard to think we can't. But to the extent that I did still believe it, was it because I'd weighed the evidence or because Josie had raised me to? Was it because giving up that belief would mean living without hope? Did I believe it the way other people believe in god and guardian angels and a higher purpose in the universe?

I could answer yes and no, passionately, to every one of those questions.

2

Summer Dawidowitz

January 2012

1

I woke up to lights, and two nurses straightening Josie's body out of the fetal curl I'd last seen her in. I said, "Oh," and they turned. A breath of understanding passed between us. It was all any of us said. One of them touched my shoulder as she headed for the door, and they left me alone in the fluorescent hospital buzz to smooth back Josie's hair, although they'd already smoothed it, and to stand beside the bed searching for one last thing I could do for her. But the face wasn't Josie's anymore. Josie had been extinguished while I was asleep and nothing I could do was ever going to reach her again.

Somewhere down the hall, a woman bellowed that she wanted to go home, she wanted to go *home*. A man said something low and soothing that I couldn't make out and the woman shouted again, louder, wilder. I thought I should go to her – if Josie had taught me anything it was to not turn away from other people's pain – but I didn't move. The woman sounded crazy and I never did know what to do with crazy. Or maybe she wasn't crazy, maybe it was just that her life was complicated. Her problems were complicated. If I walked in and asked what was wrong, she'd pour every one of them into my lap, problems cascading down, and then they'd be mine, and what the hell would I do with them? Or I'd become her new problem, the one she could solve by bellowing at me.

I can't do it, I told Josie's memory, and in the face of her silence I told myself she'd have understood. She was strategic about the problems she took on. Load the whole world's pain onto your back and it'll break you.

The woman stopped shouting. I'd dithered long enough to be excused.

I left Josie's body by itself and walked the empty hallways to the family room so I wouldn't be sitting next to her when I called the family to say she'd died. It wasn't that I thought her spirit would be hovering nearby, but I didn't want to stand next to her empty body and talk about her as if she wasn't there.

Even though she wasn't.

The TV that had spent all day grinding out news and celebs and revving car engines to soothe worried relatives was silent now and the only light came over the three-quarter wall from the corridor. Choosing the darkest corner, I knelt, lowered my head to a chair and bit its plasticky upholstered edge. In some small part of my brain, a string of cells lit up, telling me this was an odd thing to do, but it was a dim light, claiming only the tiniest fraction of my attention. To an outsider, I might have looked like I was praying, and that thought lit up a few brain cells as well. The people I come from don't pray, though. We may bite, but we do not pray.

Then I let go of the chair, dug out my phone and surrendered Josie's death to the family and all of its teeth.

*

When Zanne came through the door, I was back beside Josie's bed, worrying that the single blanket covering her might not have been enough and wanting retroactively to keep her warm. Zanne filled the room, though, driving out any thought that wasn't about her. She was impressive where any other woman in her body would've just been overweight, and she was dressed in black with a flash of silver at the neck.

"I'll wait outside," I said.

"Could we call a truce, please? Just for tonight?"

For the scantest measure of time, I weighed this. It was a physical process that bypassed thought, but nothing inside me softened, so no, apparently we couldn't. Not tonight. Not tomorrow. Not with her and not in my lifetime.

I left her there and walked the hallway until I came to the elevators, where I stopped to watch the numbers light up and go dark, and that tiny set of changes was enough to fill my mind. They lit up and went dark for some measureless length of time, then the doors opened on Jack and Raymond – my uncle and his partner.

"Summer," Raymond said, and he folded me into a hug. My head rested on the muscle below his shoulder and as I hugged him back my hand brushed his dreads. I had an impulse to braid and knot them the way I had as a kid, at first fascinated by how different they were from my own hair and, once I got past that, by all the possibilities their length offered. For a breath of time I was young enough to plaster myself to him until the empty space inside me filled. Raymond: the relative I wasn't related to; the one I could give myself over to most easily.

7

Behind me, Jack squeezed a shoulder. "You okay, kiddo?"

I pulled away to open a space for him and gathered enough of myself to say, "Zanne's in there with her."

He said, "Waiting for an audience," and then, as if the thought was connected, "I should've stayed the night. I didn't think it would happen so soon."

"I didn't think she'd be so dead."

I giggled – whatever I'd expected myself to say, it hadn't been that – then I cried and brushed my eyes almost dry.

"With Sol, I never got to see him. Josie asked if I wanted to and I wouldn't go in."

Jack squeezed my shoulder again. He was as gently rumpled as Zanne was dramatic. "Sol was pretty dead himself."

It was an oddly comforting thing to hear. In the history of the world, other people had looked at death and felt this same surprise. I stared at nothing, then the elevator doors came into focus, the metal scratched with names and hatch marks, the cock and balls boys draw on every public surface.

"Listen," Raymond said to me.

I was standing apart from him and it made him taller than when I'd leaned against him. A tree in this family of shrubs.

"About Zanne. I'd never ask you to feel anything other than what you feel, but the family has to pull together right now, and she is family. You don't have to like her and you don't have to forgive her, but you do have to be in the same room with her. You have to be in the same conversations."

He hadn't said, "She's your mother," only, "She's family," and I could accept that, but even so all I said was, "I hear you."

He raised an eyebrow to mark the difference between *I hear you* and *yes*.

8

Jack's hand was still on my shoulder, offering support, sympathy, maybe a warning. I couldn't tell which, but it was a connection and I was grateful for it.

Zanne stood looking into the dark outside Josie's window and she turned when she heard us, displaying her tearstained face. She'd never kept an emotion to herself and she'd never displayed one at its original size. She hugged Jack, pulled Raymond in, hanging on as if they were just in time to haul her from the deep.

When she released them, she asked, "What about Caro?"

Caro. Zanne and Jack's sister. My aunt. Raymond's not-quite sister-in-law. The odd one out in the family and the person I'd had in mind when I thought of the family's teeth, although our mouths were all full of them and we all knew how to use them.

"She wants us to go to her house. They're making breakfast."

We turned to Josie as if we needed to ask: was it okay if we abandoned her to this place while we fed ourselves? Jack touched her hand, a small, charged motion that made him, for some fraction of a second, beautiful, as if he'd distilled everything he knew into it, and everything he felt. I envied him that moment, as if the perfect gesture would make life bearable.

Then he moved away and he was no more than some smallish man your eye would skip over to fall in love with either Zanne or Raymond.

Raymond stepped into the same spot, touched his palm to Josie's head and whispered that she'd been a mother to him too. Silently, some seaborne giant inside me broke the surface and wept.

When Raymond moved aside, I stepped in. Why we were taking turns like this I couldn't have said. No one was on the other side of the bed and it wasn't as if she could only focus on one of us at a time. Still, it's what we did. I kissed her forehead one last time. She was a mother to me as well, but I didn't need to say so. We were closer than that.

I waited in the hallway while Zanne made her grand final gesture, and when they all filed out I followed them until at the elevators I said I'd meet them at Caro's and turned back before they had a chance to ask why.

Josie was where we'd left her – where had I thought she'd go? – and her emptiness was new enough that I narrated it to myself: *She's still here.* I lifted her hand and pressed it to my cheek, then on an impulse worked the wedding band over her knuckle, wrestling it left and right, reminding myself that I couldn't hurt her, although it felt violent all the same.

The ring came loose and I pressed her hand back to my cheek, then lowered it to the bed.

I thought the words *I'll keep this safe for you*, as if in the privacy of my head she could still hear me. This was the ring Sol had given her. She'd want it to be – what? With one of us? I didn't know and she was beyond wanting, but it felt like something I could still do for her.

My fingers closed around the ring, keeping it safe until I tucked it in my pocket, and after that there was nothing left to do but follow my family through the city's still-dark streets and across the bridge to St. Paul, with each block leaving Josie's tiny, empty body further behind.

2

JACK pushed the wreckage of his breakfast toward the center of Caro and Steve's table – a smear of egg, a film of grease, the plate as oversized as if they were running a high-end restaurant.

"Here's the question: Can I say she was a Communist?"

He was talking about the memorial, which we hadn't set a date for, but whenever we had it he wanted to be the one who'd tell her life story.

Caro groaned, although the emotion didn't go deep enough to penetrate her makeup.

"Okay, that's one vote. Anyone else?"

"It's who she was," Zanne said. "You can't tell her story without it."

Zanne, that famous advocate of unadorned fact. It gave me a floaty sense of being outside myself, just far enough away to see how surreal we all were.

"She didn't publicize it," Caro said. "Why should we have to?"

"It's not the McCarthy period anymore." Raymond's tone was gentle, as if he was offering a compromise, although he wasn't.

"We have to think about TOCK," I said. "They're the ones who could be affected by it."

TOCK was the organization Josie had founded more than half a lifetime ago, back when it really was the McCarthy period. I did fundraising for it, charging less than I charged my other clients and lying to them about it, although I expect they knew.

"How about if TOCK agrees?"

"I don't suppose it matters if I agree," Caro said.

Jack held his fork in both hands as if he was testing the handle. It was expensive, yes, but would it bend?

"It won't hurt you in any material way," he said. "It could hurt the organization."

"Is that what matters? Material ways?"

"It's who she was," Zanne said again.

"Right. So we've decided then: We're going to tell everybody everything that ever happened in the family. We're going to drag them through every miserable bit of history we've got."

"Who said it was miserable?"

Since it was Zanne asking, I said, "You might have noticed I wasn't exactly happy."

Zanne got as far as "That's—" but Jack talked over her and she used it as a get-out-of-jail-free card.

"This isn't any random bit of history. It's not the difference between blue hair ribbons and green ones."

"I didn't say it was hair ribbons."

"Just tell 'em," Zanne said, trying to stare me down as if I'd been the one saying we shouldn't mention it. "Fuck 'em if they don't like it."

Quietly, more as if he was thinking out loud than criticizing, Steve said, "Elegantly put."

"I'll say it in Latin if you like."

I waited to see if he'd take her up on the offer.

"Everyone, please." Raymond turned one palm up like someone checking for rain.

"Oh, do what you like," Caro said. "You will anyway."

Steve touched Caro's arm. Silent speech in the language of the long-married. *Your family's crazy*, it said. *You can't change them.*

"More coffee," Caro said, making it more of a command than a question. "Summer, what about toast? You could eat that much."

"I can't."

She extended the platter anyway – something seeded and buttered, from Whole Foods if I'd had to guess. It was nutritious, overpriced and repellent. I couldn't understand how these relatives of mine were eating while Josie lay so completely dead, but Caro and Steve had set out enough bacon, eggs, fruit and toast to feed a small village, and the leftovers were congealing on the serving platters. When we left, they'd scrape it all down the garbage disposal to feed the rats that live in the sewers. Rats in rich neighborhoods live better than the global poor. It's trickle-down economics at work.

My hands had made themselves into a barricade.

"You're sure?"

Steve lifted the plate from her hands and set it back on the table.

"Caro, she said no." He took the coffee pot and left us.

"You'll sing?" Raymond asked Zanne.

13

The question was as kind as it was unnecessary. We'd have had to drug her to keep her from singing, but she wanted someone to ask. *Needed* someone to ask.

"Just for god's sake don't sing 'Beloved Comrade,'" Caro said.

Zanne leaned an elbow on the table, smiled and sang directly at her.

To you, beloved comrade,
We make this solemn vow:
The fight will go on.
The fight will still go on.

She'd started it on a low note, close to the bottom of her range, and when her voice lifted she broke the song into open grief.

Rest here in the earth,
Your work is done,
You'll find new birth
When we have won.
When we have won.

It undid me. From as far back as I can remember, her voice always could undo me, even though her solemnest vows were nothing more than trained air. The fight – what Josie always called the struggle, although it had too many syllables to make its way into the song – vibrated in the room with Josie's children, their partners, her one lone grandchild, who she'd raised herself because her daughter got distracted. Carried on Zanne's voice, the struggle wasn't either terrifying or some long, daily slog, but the state we most longed to enter. Red nirvana. Satori. Love itself.

Then the song ended and Jack gave a shudder, half theatrical, half – I think – real. "It's overblown, I know it's overblown, but god, it is so beautiful."

The song was slow to let go of us, and it echoed into a silence until Steve – wide-shouldered, quiet, unknowable – came back with the coffee and we got back to work, listing the people who had to be told, deciding who'd make which calls. Steve refilled my cup, his free hand resting on my shoulder. I'd always sensed a gentleness about the man, even though I had only the vaguest idea of who he was. He'd been in my life since I was five, like some kindly piece of furniture. Raymond had made himself a part of the family, but Steve stood aside. If lightning struck us, he'd be safe.

"Can we call you for phone numbers?" Jack asked me. "You know where she kept her phone book?"

Of course I knew. I knew every detail of her last year. I knew she'd eaten crackers in bed when she couldn't sleep, knew that in the morning she'd vacuumed crumbs off the sheet until she couldn't manage the vacuum anymore, at which point I took over, because crazy as it was, it was easier than brushing crumbs onto the floor and vacuuming them there.

None of the rest of them knew this, only me. Me, me, me, humming the same tune as Zanne and Caro.

How did Josie and Sol give rise to this nest of me-creatures? How had Jack managed to slip free?

"Or email," I said. "Whatever's easier."

15

"What about the obit?" Caro asked. "You want to write it now? I could do it later."

Before the idea of Caro writing it could gain traction, Jack started to dictate: "Josephine Freund Dawidowitz. Born, died, survived by. Include husband and partners."

Caro made notes.

"What about David?" Zanne asked.

"He is family," Caro said, her pen hovering.

"Not anymore he isn't," Jack said.

"Josie didn't count him in," I said.

That made it two to one, and we turned to Zanne, the wild card in our pack, to see if she'd deadlock us.

"Leave him out," she said, not bothering to justify her vote.

"Retouching history again," Caro said.

Raymond put a hand on Jack's arm to stop him from arguing.

I half remembered a story from Stalin's time about one of the old Bolsheviks who'd been airbrushed out of a photo when he fell from favor. If they had airbrushes then. Maybe they did it by hand. Maybe I was mistaking metaphor for fact.

"Founder of TOCK," Jack said.

"Have to spell it out."

"Spell it out, then."

Their voices were sharp and short, threatening a spat about even this.

"Founder of Teach Our Children."

Caro paced the words barely ahead of her pen.

When they first chose the name, Josie'd wanted to leave out the *K* because it didn't stand for anything, but she lost the vote. Decades later, when it was just the two of us, she still sometimes called it "TOCK-the-K-is-silent."

"How much do they charge for these things?" Zanne asked.

"From each according to their ability," Jack said. "We'll split it fairly."

We'd had this discussion before, when Josie's bills outran her income, and after a few squabbles about how able some of us were, we didn't do badly.

"Want the abbreviation too?"

"That's all some people know it as." Another time where I got to be the expert. Me, me, me.

"Parentheses TOCK."

"Blacklisted as a teacher during the McCarthy era for her political activity. That should come before the first mention of TOCK."

Caro wouldn't repeat this but she wrote, her fingers tight and angry on the pen.

"Any memorials should be made to TOCK?"

Even Caro nodded. Anything else would be heresy. I could have told her it wasn't a politically challenging organization, but she already knew that and it didn't bail any water out of a childhood she alone saw as leaky. Josie had put politics before Caro. She'd put TOCK before Caro.

Poor Caro. None of the rest of us thought Josie had shortchanged us.

The discussion moved on. Cremation. The memorial again. Her will, because even the purest of us accumulate things. She'd left the house to the four of us equally and trusted us to divide its contents without spilling blood. We

17

dealt out the tasks like playing cards and there was something comforting about knowing we had jobs to do, decisions to make – the unsentimental business of living on after someone dies.

"I brought her ring," I said.

In my imagination, fishing it out of my pocket was going to be seamless, but the reality was awkward. I had to separate it from the change I carried, then my hand caught in my pocket and I half stood to pull it out. Caro said "Keep it" while I was still struggling.

I set the ring on the table. This was what I'd brought and this was what I was going to deliver.

Jack picked it up, held it a moment, his hand forming a cushion for it to rest on, then gave it back.

"Keep it," he said. "Someone has to."

3

By the time we broke up, the night of Josie's death had opened into a steel-gray morning, and I took a moment to stand alone on the sidewalk, pulling cold air into my lungs, letting its sharp edges clear the family from my body, reassembling the adult I could only manage to be in their absence.

Caro and Steve lived a block and a half from Summit Avenue, as close as they could afford to the turn-of-the-century grace the robber barons had left behind and the upper middle class now nested in. It was a well-behaved neighborhood, with an underlying tension about how close it sat to – they'd whisper it so as not to risk offending anyone – the Black neighborhood along the freeway.

Not that they were prejudiced, mind you.

Their block had a bland kind of beauty, and for a second or two I was grateful for its quiet.

Then I drove home, and I'd closed Josie's garage door and was headed for the back gate when Irene crossed the alley toward me, dressed for work, looking both tough and office-ready, a cigarette in one hand, a purse big enough to hold a kitchen chair over the opposite shoulder.

"Any news on your gramma?"

"Gone, Irene. Early this morning."

Instead of saying she was sorry, she said, "She was a real lady, you know?"

I laughed. Because it was true. Because none of us get to escape our history. Because Josie never stopped carrying herself like she knew where the goodies were kept. She'd have trained that out of herself if she'd known a way, but she'd absorbed it too young.

Irene gave me a one-armed hug, holding the cigarette to one side, protecting my shoulder blades from the smoke. It was awkward. She'd sat with Josie when things got to the point where I didn't feel right leaving her alone, but we'd never been on hugging terms.

She smelled of stale tobacco and winter air.

"Stop by if you want company," she said. "Have a beer. A cup of coffee. Whatever."

I said I would. They were the things people say – stop by; I will – one side not knowing if the invitation's welcome, the other not knowing if it's real, both of us wondering if we didn't like each other best with an alley in between.

"I gotta run. I'll miss my bus."

She was half a garage length away before I called my thanks after her. She waved an arm to say she'd heard, but she didn't turn.

Josie's house was quieter than the 3 a.m. hospital corridors had been. If Irene hadn't just left for work, I'd have run back out and asked her in. I wanted someone there to breathe

the air with me. The words of a song, or as many of them as I could get hold of, echoed in my head: *Old someone's dead and gone, left me here to sing this song.* Until that moment, I would have thought that was a single state, dead and gone, but it wasn't. In the hospital, Josie had been dead. Here, though, in the house I'd shared with her, she was gone, an absence so big it swallowed the possibility of sound. It was a different thing altogether. I traced a path from the kitchen to the dining room to the living room, opening curtains, bringing in the winter light.

In each room, her absence echoed off the walls.

Old Josie's dead and gone, left me here to sing this song.

I tried to clear the words out of my head. It was like sweeping smoke until I substituted "Beloved Comrade". Jack was right about it being overblown, and he was also right that it was beautiful. I sang most of the first line before my voice broke and I wept. For Josie. For her long-lost comrades – that poisoned, antiquated, beloved word. It wasn't a word she'd used, and even in my thoughts I never had. One or two of her – let's say it – comrades actually had talked about each other as comrades, although I never heard them say "Hello, comrade", or anything that embarrassing. It was more like "Some of the comrades were there", and even that didn't happen often. I doubt I'd heard it used half a dozen times. Just enough to remind me that even if it doesn't fit comfortably on an American tongue, it had once been a living part of the language. They'd meant it. Or some of them had.

As far as I know, the Communist Party had already folded in on itself by the time I heard anyone put breath behind the word. The Soviet Union had collapsed, leaving these old warriors behind to remind each other of who they'd been and what they'd hoped for. To trade news of the small battle fires they still tended. To tell each other about their aches, their illnesses, their grandkids, their disappointments. Josie had loved them, and they drove her crazy with their complaining.

I was weeping partly for Josie and partly for all the purity that might have made the world a better place and hadn't.

When I ran out of tears, I picked up the shoes she'd left by her chair, knobbed where her bunions had fought the leather for space, and I carried them to her closet and lined them up neatly, as if she might need them again. Then I turned the covers down on one side of her bed and curled myself into it.

Josie's sheets were older than I was, but they were good cotton – percale, she told me once – and they'd grown softer with age until now they were as smooth as skin. She'd committed her life to the working class, but she'd kept a weakness for small luxuries. Like Irene said, she was a lady.

When I was little, she used to sing me a song about a lord's wife who runs off with the Gypsies and says she won't miss her husband's goose-feather bed. She'll sleep in a cold, open field. I used to think of it as Josie's story, only she ended up with the best of both worlds: Sol and the cold, open world, plus two sets of damn fine sheets.

Only I didn't know back then how good Josie's sheets were. Which was just as well, because I was a little purist and would've looked down my nose at them, and at her for having them. I didn't find out about them until I moved back in to help with those small, essential jobs like vacuuming crumbs off them.

The day she went into the hospital, I put clean sheets on the bed to welcome her home, folding them down the way she taught me to, so the piping showed above the blankets. The way the lord's sheets are turned down: bravely-o. Even though I half knew she wasn't coming back.

Or – admit it – I hoped she wasn't. She'd been wanting to die ever since the strokes robbed her of the person she'd been. If humans had an off button, she'd have pushed hers. It was an act of love to want her death, and wishing for it had left me fouled.

I didn't exactly sleep in her bed, but I lay there, my mind hazed, wanting her back as helplessly as I'd ever wanted Zanne to come back for me, and I let time pass until the phone rang and Caro asked for a couple of people's numbers. Then Jack wanted a few, and when I hung up I made my own calls: Josie, early this morning, we wanted you to know, we'll call about the memorial as soon as we get it figured out, although it won't be right away. And yes, we'll miss her. We'll all miss her.

I spread my grief across the city until it was wide and thin and damn near bearable.

When I couldn't think of anything else to do with myself, I called Shar and told her how much I missed her. I didn't tell her Josie was dead. I had a half-formed sense that telling her on the phone would cheapen it and a less-than-half-formed sense that once I told her, my grief wouldn't be my own any-more, so I held it close. This belonged to no one but me, even while she was the one person I wanted comfort from.

She asked if I could come over, meaning could someone stay with Josie, and I said I could, not telling her we were past that and had been for days.

I felt the Household's gravity pulling at me.

The Household, capital H, meant Shar, Tee and Zac. Before Josie reached the point where she couldn't live alone, it had meant the three of them plus me, although I was never in the inner orbit. I was a moon circling Shar. But even after a year of making my bed at Josie's and keeping most of my stuff there, I still thought of it as *the* Household, as if it was the only one I knew of.

I unlocked their front door and walked into the full scream of the vacuum. Shar caught sight of me and fumbled for the power button, yelling over the noise for me to wait, reminding me of someone struggling with a dog that outweighed her. She hit the button and the scream curved downward into silence.

"Hey," she said.

She was still holding the vacuum and couldn't seem to free herself from it.

"Josie died," I said. "Last night." I stood at the edge of the rug, hands inside my jacket pockets, each one clutching a glove.

She leaned the vacuum wand against the wall and we watched it slide, neither of us making a move to catch it, flinching in unison when it clattered on the floor, as if the sound had surprised us. As if Josie's death had. She moved toward me and I shook my head, saying no to something: No, don't be kind to me. Don't cry, don't touch, don't speak, although what had I come there for if not all of that?

"It's what she'd been wanting. Since the first stroke."

It felt right to say this, as if I owed Josie bluntness.

"All the same," she said.

She told me to take off my jacket, and it seemed natural that she had to tell me this.

"Here. Sit."

I let her park me on the couch and she sat next to me.

"I'll miss her," she said.

I thought the words *I know you will* but couldn't say them. She'd known Josie since we were kids, and that helped anchor me to the planet. We held hands for some time before we turned toward each other. She touched her forehead to mine, laying her hand across the back of my neck, and we rested there until something inside me opened to her – an unquestionably physical feeling that didn't match any physical event and was more intimate than any kiss I've ever known. I spread my hand across the back of her neck in an echo of her hand on mine and my mind stopped pumping out thoughts, just marveled at the wave of feeling that lifted us.

And then, slowly, it set us down. I folded back into myself. She folded back into hers. We kissed, light and sweet, and we separated.

"You want to go upstairs?" I asked.

I hadn't known sex could grow out of the same ground as loss, but it did, and I followed her up the stairs to her room.

By the time we came back down, Tee was folding laundry on the living room floor. She stood, a single motion like a dancer's, until she was upright, a sunflower blossoming between the stacked underwear and the laundry basket. Even stock-still, she had a grace about her. Then she hugged me, rocking me left and right.

"Josie died," I said into her shoulder.

Her grip tightened.

"Oh, Summer."

Her voice had gone teary, as if the loss was hers, although of the three Household members she'd known Josie the least. I squeezed back long enough to be polite, then extricated myself. I didn't want to cry. I didn't want anyone else to cry, especially Tee, whose tears were—

It wasn't that they were easy. They wrenched her hard on their way out, but she had too many, and too many things set them flowing. If she cried now, it wouldn't be for Josie, it would be because the world's grief overran her sometimes. Once, before Josie's stroke, when I still lived with the Household, I came home late and found her weeping in the dark over a woman she'd seen at first light, collecting cans from the alley before the recycling truck came, pushing them in a supermarket cart that was hung with black bags. She carried a stick with a nail at the end to scare away dogs. Or people. Tee had a couple of bucks on her and she gave it to the woman, who tucked it in her bra and moved on. Tee hadn't, though. She was still weeping. She should've had more, given more, done more. Instead, she felt more.

I sat with Tee for a while that night, telling her she was a good person, but it wasn't what she needed to hear, and it wasn't what I wanted to say either. Because what good did her tears do the woman in the alley?

They wouldn't do me any good either. This wasn't her fucking pain, it was mine, and I wasn't sharing.

"It's okay," I heard myself say, and to soften it I added what I'd said to Shar: "It's what she wanted."

It came as a kind of footnote.

I followed Shar to the kitchen, where she put a pan on the stove and poured in leftover soup, and I was prepared to believe I could eat. It wasn't Caro's overpriced health food. I was back in the life I'd chosen, and I watched her stir the soup. She was a small woman with yarn-wrapped, white-girl dreads. They were different in texture, in width, in message from Raymond's. He didn't approve of white people wearing dreads but he'd been generous enough to stop saying so when she sprouted hers, although that didn't keep me from remembering it.

She set bowls on the table and called Tee. I stirred mine: carrots, beans, whole wheat macaroni. There'd be miso in there somewhere – there was always miso – and it was crammed with protein and fiber and alternatives to capitalism. I stared into it as if I could read our entire philosophical mix inside my chipped, flowery bowl, but I didn't spoon it into my body. Instead I told them about the hospital, the nurses, everything I now knew about pneumonia. I stirred the soup, making the acquaintance of a new bean, a different slice of carrot. "Beloved Comrade" came back to me. Josie wouldn't have counted miso as a weapon in the struggle, and I had to admit she had a point. It wasn't the magic enzyme that would break down capitalism.

"Zanne showed up," I said.

"How'd it go?" Shar asked.

"It's been worse. Mostly she let me ignore her."

She sang, the voice inside me said, but I didn't want to talk about the layers of meaning – or if not meaning, at least feeling – involved in that. I didn't understand them anyway. Instead, I said, "I've been thinking all morning about how sure Josie and Sol were that history led to the revolution and that life would be better afterwards."

Shar hummed an acknowledgment.

I said, "I envy them that."

Even if they were wrong? the voice inside me asked.

Fuck yes. Even then.

My housemates – this odd family of mine – talked about revolution more than Josie or Sol ever had. They reminded me of myself as a kid, dreaming about Che Guevara, guns, the mountains – whichever the hell mountains I thought he'd fought in. I'm not sure I even knew what country he was in. I knew he was dead, but that didn't strike me as a problem. I still imagined joining up.

The romance of revolution. Revolution as a goal of its own.

Josie and Sol didn't talk about revolution as some cleansing wave that would solve every problem, and they didn't expect it in their lifetimes – not in this country. They focused on their small slice of world and on its problems. Josie worked to improve the schools the way someone else might clean the house, knowing the dirt would come back, taking pleasure where she could, doing what needed to be done even where she couldn't.

The only time I remember her saying "come the revolution", it was as part of a joke: "'Come the revolution, comrade, we'll all have peaches and cream.'

"'But I don't like peaches and cream.'

"'Come the revolution, comrade, you'll like peaches and cream.'"

So she'd used the word *comrade* as well as *revolution*. Twice each, but in a joke.

A decent world. That was the phrase she used. Over and over. In a decent world—

Shar was telling Tee about Josie, the impact she'd had on her as a kid. The legend of Josie Freund Dawidowitz. Here was this woman who didn't pretend to be any less strong than she was. Who didn't apologize for herself.

"I didn't really get her politics till later, but I remember the way she talked to us – a couple of eight-year-olds, maybe ten-year-olds. As if we were adults."

I stirred my soup, said hello to a bit of unpeeled, anti-consumerist carrot. It was full of the cooperative spirit and if only I could have eaten it, it would have started building a better world inside me.

I couldn't. I pushed the bowl away as Zac blew through the back door on a blast of cold air, stomping a memory of snow from his boots even though the sidewalks were clear, announcing his presence with his feet, filling the room. He leaned in to kiss the top of Shar's head. She pulled him down for a real kiss, then let him go so he could kiss Tee's head, then mine, working his way around the table. Equal warmth. Almost equal familiarity. Cold cheek, cold jacket. Zac and I didn't love each other the way we would have if we'd been lovers, although there was love between us. I'd have said as if we were like brother and sister, but I'd been with my family too recently to think I could coax emotional cash out of that

29

machine. Like an old couple, then, who'd put sex behind them, although sex had never been a possibility for us. He and Shar were lovers, and so were he and Tee. It didn't take anything away from me, even if in the beginning I'd thought it would.

Usually it didn't take anything away from me.

Mostly it didn't.

He grabbed a paper towel from the counter, honked into it, shoved it in his pocket.

When we first moved in together, we argued about whether to buy paper towels and agreed not to, but someone always did, and Zac always used them as kleenex, which we did agree to buy – not the actual brand but the woody, recycled ones the co-op sold. Maybe paper towels struck him as less bourgeois, even if, one for one, they used up more of the world's resources.

"Hey, we miss you," he said to me.

"Josie died," Tee told him. It was a reminder, a warning: Other people have feelings unrelated to yours. The warning was as unrelated to my feelings as Zac's breeziness was. It was like being handed a woody, recycled box of kleenex when you're not crying.

"Oh." A downward slide from happy to sober.

"Last night," she said, that edge of tears back in her voice.

Zac said "oh" again, slipping all the way to somber, but he couldn't hold himself there and he grinned. "Hey, remember when we took her to the Occupy camp?"

Without consulting me, my face grinned back at him. It was an odd feeling, as if I'd pasted the grin on slantwise.

We'd gone to the Occupy camp just after the family got Josie a wheelchair, and I suggested the trip with the hazy idea that it would keep her engaged with the world. In a different family, they might take the old lady shopping, or get her hair done. In mine, we took her to a demonstration.

Even then I knew it wouldn't help, but how many of us, when some scary bit of our bodies goes wrong, don't throw everything we know about medicine out the window and try willpower and magical messaging? Besides, I'd been feeling sorry for myself. The struggle for a decent world, that great romantic goal of my childhood, was breaking out all over the six o'clock news, and I was sitting on my ass writing grant applications while Josie nodded off over the newspaper and woke up to ask for the fifty-seventh time if I knew where Zanne was and whether the house was too warm for me. I'd long since stopped wanting to know where Zanne was and the house was past too warm and solidly in the hot zone, but Josie would freeze if I turned the thermostat down. Meanwhile, Shar, Zac and Tee were fizzing with news from the Occupy camp. They'd slept there while the wind blew straight down off the Canadian plains. They'd scrounged sleeping bags somewhere and left them for whoever needed them. They cooked food, brought anarchist literature for the library tent. They joined discussions about everything from how to keep the food warm to the true meaning of democracy. Nothing was too small, nothing was too big, and nothing – from what I could tell on my overheated perch in front of the computer screen – was ever settled. It was anarchist democracy in action, they told me. No one who'd been touched by it would ever be the same, and even though I wasn't an anarchist I was prepared to think they might be onto something. Occupy camps were popping up like whack-a-moles all around the globe. Zac swore the 99 per cent had found a voice, and wouldn't you know, I was missing the whole damn conversation.

Josie agreed to go when I suggested it, but her voice stayed flat.

"We don't have to," I said.

"We'll go."

Again that flatness, as if she was discussing fate itself. Words were hard to come by after her stroke, and she didn't waste them.

It took both Zac and me to load the wheelchair into the trunk, plus Tee to stand behind us and kibitz.

Now that I wouldn't need the skill anymore, I could load it single-handed in a quarter of the time, without wrenching my back.

We drove downtown and plugged a parking meter. It was a deeply un-Occupy act, at least as I understood it, but the alternatives were to park in a ramp or let ourselves get a ticket, both of which would cost more, so I fed my coins in and we rolled Josie to the barren plaza where the occupation had set up its huddle of tents, its signs and tarps. Minneapolis wasn't New York or Madrid. It wasn't even Oakland. We were a small Midwestern city, with a relatively well-behaved occupation made up of people who wished they lived someplace more important.

Or maybe it was only me. Maybe they were proud of it.

A couple of drummers pounded on plastic buckets. Two women who might have been in their late teens wrestled with the lines on a drooping tent, and a man with a gray beard and a thin ponytail came out of the information tent to greet us.

He was a fixture on the left, someone whose roots were in the Vietnam-era anti-war movement, and Josie would have known him before her stroke but she wasn't the same person now, so I introduced him. He apologized for the low numbers. Evenings were busier, he said, and anyway, a number of people were in court today, supporting someone or other who'd been arrested. He said the name as if we'd know her. Last night there'd been thirty people at the general meeting. The night before, there'd been fifty.

I couldn't tell how much Josie was taking in.

We did a quick tour of the tents, and when we got back to where we'd started Zac leaned down from behind Josie's wheelchair.

"Here it is, Josie: This is the revolution."

A moment's pause while she searched for words.

"It's going to take more than this."

I was embarrassed for Zac, and at the same time I had an urge to defend him. Yes, he was silly, but weren't radical politics kind of like love? If no one risked looking silly, nothing happened.

Sitting at the kitchen table, though, that wasn't the moment he reminded us of. He picked up the moment just afterward, when Tee held up a sign someone had propped against a tent, CAN I HAVE MY FUTURE BACK, PLEASE?, and Josie laughed – a bitter-edged, we-have-to-laugh-anyway sound, a touch of the woman she'd once been.

So Zac remembered a tiny triumph while I held onto absurdity. Or failure.

"Any soup left?" he asked.

I pushed my bowl across the table.

"Take mine."

"Don't. I'll find something else."

"I'm not eating. I'm just stirring it around and sightseeing."

"You sure?"

But already he'd pulled it toward himself.

"You coming back to us, then?"

I'd have preferred it if Shar had asked this, and she would have eventually, but that was what happened with Zac in the room: we took a step back and he moved forward to fill the space. Or maybe he started out in front. The dealings between the women took place in the background, in a language he couldn't quite catch – one he didn't stop talking long enough to learn. How was it I'd never known that? It was as if I'd been living by a river all my life and had only now noticed water. There we were, thinking we could change the world, while we mindlessly recreated the one we'd grown up in.

I said, "That's the plan," but I didn't sound as warm about it as I'd expected to.

Shar touched my hand, unknotting something inside me, and when the moment ended she carried her bowl to the sink. On the way back, she traced the curve of Zac's ear with one finger. I listened for the squeak of jealousy but heard only the echoey sound of distance.

In the obit she was writing, Caro would list Shar as my partner and not mention Zac or Tee, and that would be both accurate and a deliberate misunderstanding. I could have told her to list them and, however uneasily, she would have. I hadn't, though, and I wasn't going to. That seemed sad and inevitable and worth noticing.

Rob wandered up from the basement, where he'd been working on who knows what. A salvaged bike. A broken toaster. He was our Occupy nomad. Right up to the end, with the bitterest weather closing in, he'd lived at the camp as close to full-time as a person could stand to, and he took refuge in the bedroom I wasn't using when he needed a break. When the city finally sent cops to break up the camp, I couldn't help thinking, from the safety of my computer chair, that it was an act of mercy, even though it wasn't meant to be. Now the camp was gone, Rob lived at the house and worked for Occupy Homes – a descendant of the encampment that tried to keep banks from foreclosing on people's houses. He'd been arrested twice already for blocking repossessions.

Zac picked up the coffee pot, offered it in Rob's direction, and Rob said sure, he'd love some.

"That's older than I am," Shar said.

"That's okay. All I need is the kick. You want a fresh pot?"

Rob shook his head. If it had been made, he'd use it up. If a cicada had jumped in and drowned, he'd have called it a protein boost.

It wasn't cicada season. Zac poured coffee into the cup Rob held out and a charge ran between them. In a sexually liberated straight man's sort of way, Zac was in love with Rob. He wanted to pour him coffee, make him laugh, get him to write "this is brilliant" on his test paper, only we were grown now, we didn't take tests and Rob wasn't his teacher, but that didn't change the wanting. Rob could have been one of the early twentieth century's hobo-organizers – Joe Hill with a laptop and a cell phone instead of a freight train, a song and a union. He owned two pairs of jeans, some long johns, a sweater and a backpack. Okay, that wasn't a full count – he also had a good down-filled jacket someone had donated to the Occupation, and it came with gloves, a scarf and a hat, plus whatever bits and pieces I hadn't seen, but it could all have fit in the back seat of a small borrowed car and still leave room for hitchhikers. If Zac had been ten years younger, if he hadn't found a job that suited his politics, if he hadn't been part of this patchwork family of ours, these were the choices he'd have made.

Or thought he'd have made. It's always easier to wish you could cut yourself adrift than it is to take your knife to the anchor rope.

Zac poured them both enough milk to mask the taste of aging coffee and told Rob Josie had died.

"She was an inspiration," Rob said, and Zac echoed that she was.

I nodded without saying that if they'd belonged to Josie's generation they'd have been on opposite sides in the old Communist/anarchist battles over whether a tightly disciplined party could free anyone or a wild network of free-associating individuals could overthrow anything larger than a dumpster, not to mention whether it could replace it with something better than mayhem. But the age gap and the limits on what she was able to say during the time Rob had known her let him ignore all that. She'd become a generic lefty icon: someone who'd stayed true to her beliefs.

And in fairness, Rob's politics weren't Zac's or Shar's. I wasn't sure if he was an anarchist, or for that matter what anarchism was anymore. Was it a philosophy? A dozen philosophies? A way to give the respectable world the finger?

Hell, I wasn't sure what socialism was either. A much-needed if unspecified alternative to capitalism. How much time did I have before anyone needed the details?

"You ready to have your room back?" Rob asked. "Because I can move on. Or take the couch for a while if no one minds."

"I don't want to put you out."

"It's not a problem. You've been fantastic."

"I've got a bunch of stuff to wind up at Josie's. I'll let you know, okay?"

He said great, then asked if anyone wanted the bathroom before he ran himself a bath. When no one did, he left us.

Zac carried the bowls to the sink, washed them and balanced them on top of the stack already in the dish drainer, and we sat for a while, talking about nothing in particular, just being together. After a while, Rob came downstairs and showed me video clips from the Occupation, then clips from bigger Occupations around the world: Oakland, Madrid, New York, London. This was Rob being sociable. He didn't do chat.

I lost track of location, of time, of whether any of them were still going on. Meetings ran in an endless loop. We sat on the couch, knees pointing toward each other, laptop balanced on his left, on my right. Demonstrators marched away from a camp somewhere, walked until the police scattered them, marched again. It was happening earlier, or later, or all over again, or someplace else. This is what I'd missed while I was taking care of Josie. Maybe it was because Josie had just died and I wasn't quite present, but not being able to tell what was still going on and what wasn't made it all seem as insubstantial as air. It so completely wasn't the revolution.

The Household, a small voice inside me said, *isn't the revolution either.*

Everything that's solid melts into air, Marx wrote somewhere, although not in anything I remember reading, it was one of those quotes that had shaken loose from his endless pages of text until it worked its way down to my half-educated self.

He probably wasn't referring to the Household.

Zac went upstairs. Tee stacked her laundry in the basket, set it on the chair and wandered off without it.

Rob could have shown me clips all day and into the night, but the house was closing in on me. I put a hand on his shoulder and said, "Another time, yeah?"

I found Shar upstairs and told her I needed some time at Josie's. I needed to organize my stuff and Josie's stuff, not to mention my life and Josie's death. I'd said more or less the same thing when Rob asked about moving back, and she'd heard it then, but something was pushing me to say it to her, to say it for her, and by way of apology to paint more detail into the picture.

She said she understood and hugged me tight enough that I almost stayed.

I was suiting up to step into the cold, thin air outside the spaceship that was our house – the jacket, the scarf, the hat, the gloves – when Zac clattered downstairs to catch me.

"Hey, I was thinking I'd do some target practice before work tomorrow. You want to come?"

I looked at him blankly.

"Target practice?" He made rifle motions. "Pshew, pshew?"
He mimed a tiny recoil on each *pshew*.

"I thought Shar would've told you."

I shook my head.

"It's, you know, it's something we should be learning. So I found this gun range. It's—"

He gave a small laugh.

"Yeah. The politics would make your hair catch fire, but why should right-wing nutjobs be the only people who know their way around a gun? We need this. Can you come?"

I shook my head for a while before words came.

"Got a shitload of things to do."

"Another time, then? We really do need to know this stuff."

"Another time," I said, not because I meant to go but because talking to Zac was like that. If I didn't have my feet solidly planted, I'd get dragged along after him.

4

THAT night was long and shallow, but eventually morning came, as morning will if you wait long enough, and I made a piece of toast and found I could eat it. I drank coffee, sitting in my old place at the kitchen table – the one that had been mine when I was little and Sol was still alive, the one I kept after he died and it was just me and Josie, even though it meant we sat kitty-corner instead of opposite each other. As if either of us moving would have diminished our memory of him.

When I moved back in with her, I took my old spot.

Josie's pill bottles were still tumbled in the woven basket Jack and Raymond had given her, and I ran a finger over its edge. They would've found it at some street fair, or seen it in a store window, the black background sharpening the flashes of red and green, and even if they didn't know about her sheets, they knew Josie's weakness for the small, beautiful things of this world and they loved her not in spite of her weaknesses but because of them.

The kitchen needed a coat of paint. The whole house needed a coat of paint. Before Josie's stroke, Caro had wanted to pay a painter but Josie'd held her off. Too much disruption. And it didn't seem to matter anymore.

Even then, she was counting the time to her expiration date.

I could take the bottles out of the basket now, toss them in a drawer, maybe throw them in the trash. They were no more use to Josie, and while she was alive I'd hated that her fingers couldn't manage the lids, leaving me to open them for her and dole out the markers of her decay. Here's one for blood pressure, one for glaucoma, one for depression and why wouldn't she be depressed, with or without the pills?

I wanted Josie back, and I couldn't help thinking she'd been smart to get out.

To hell with the pill bottles. I left them where they were and made my own smaller escape, abandoning my dishes in the sink, settling into the dining room, where I'd moved my computer so I could be near Josie while I worked. Piles of paper had surrounded it, I swear, of their own accord and formed a layer of protection around me.

I reviewed my deadlines. Work had gone thin in the past year and the only thing looming over me was the need to pick up more work. Money was as thin as work was. I answered a few emails, signed a few petitions, wondering if they made any difference, dumped the spam and the endless requests for donations. I didn't pack up my stuff to move back into the Household. Instead I convened a meeting in my head and agreed to spend the morning at the computer. Before Josie went into the hospital, I'd been working on a grant application for the battered women's shelter, and it was almost done. When Zac's number came up on my phone, I let the call roll into voicemail. When Shar called, I watched the phone and thought about answering, and I thought about it long enough that the call met Zac's in the Great Hall of Unanswered Messages.

It was late morning when Zanne rang the doorbell, wanting Josie's address book, and of course she hadn't called the people on her list yesterday. It wouldn't cross her mind that people should hear about it from us directly. Or if it did, their needs would weigh less than her own. I told her she could make her calls from Josie's room. I didn't want her there, but if she'd gotten out of the house with the address book we'd never have seen it again. She'd set it down at a friend's, or drop it in a Goodwill box and tell me in all innocence that she hadn't known it mattered, or knew it mattered but thought she was dropping something else in. A frying pan whose nonstick layer was coming unstuck. An earring whose mate had set up housekeeping in some other city. A daughter needing a more reliable home.

She kicked off her shoes and stretched out on Josie's remade bed, and I went back to the computer and worked at not listening to her, but I never could shut her voice out. It flowed down the scrap of hallway that ran between the downstairs bedrooms and it turned the corner to the dining room. Not for the first time, I wished the computer was back upstairs.

"She was," Zanne said into the phone. "She really was," and even though I couldn't know what she was agreeing with, her voice wheelbarrowed a load of loss into my belly and dumped it there.

I sent an email or two, opened and closed files, made all the motions I made when I was working, although I wasn't, and in the blank space where work should have been, my few deadlines grew until they pressed against each other and I seemed to have more work than two of me could manage.

Eventually Zanne made her last call, throwing a final emotion through the wires, probably at someone who felt real grief and didn't need hers. She leaned in the doorway and watched me ignore her.

"Let me make you a cup of coffee," she said. "Let's spend some time together."

"Had some. I'm working."

She sighed.

The grant application stared at me from the screen, but it was pointless to pretend I could work with her watching. I spun my chair.

"You remember work? That thing people do when they have to get paid?"

"I've heard rumors about it, yes."

She was posed against the hinge side of the doorway, too old for sexy and too broad for fashion, but her body knew its power, and it made her beautiful. Not because of any inherent beauty but because of her sheer damn comfort in herself. She might as well have been onstage.

No, she was onstage. She was always onstage.

"I won't take much of your time. I have something I need to tell you."

The question *Why do I let her do this to me?* scrolled across my mind like a storm warning at the bottom of the TV screen. An impossible mother warning. But even while I asked the question, I was standing up to make coffee so she wouldn't get the chance. The house might not belong to me any more than it did to her, but I lived here, so I'd boil the water, thank you, and I'd measure the coffee and push down the plunger and thump two mugs and the milk carton on the table.

I wouldn't have minded a cookie, but I wasn't going to set them out to share with her.

So there.

We sat at the kitchen table like boxers, measuring each other's weaknesses. I wondered where she was staying but didn't ask. The question sounded friendlier, when I heard it in my head, than I was willing to be. Besides, I was used to not knowing, and Josie wouldn't be asking anymore.

"Okay, that's coffee. Now what?"

"Yes, hello, Summer, it's a joy to see you too."

"Hello, Zanne. I'm comatose with delight. Now tell me what you have to say, drink your coffee, and let me get some work done."

"It's too hot to drink."

"That happens to water when you boil it."

"You drink your coffee this hot, you get cancer of the esophagus."

"Oh, for fuck's sake. Run some cold in it. Add more milk. You're the one who wanted coffee."

She spread her hands, palms facing me to form a backstop, as if they could protect her from whatever I might say next.

"Look—" she said, but couldn't find anything to follow it.

A seed of pity pushed up a shoot. Here she was, this single time, without words, without promises, sitting raw and awkward across the table from her life's great failure.

Even in that, she'd have to be outsized. I couldn't be just her failure, I'd have to be her great one.

44

"Zanne—"

But I'd run out of words myself. All I knew was what I didn't want: the two of us in some weepy scene of forgiveness. We'd had enough of those when I was a kid. She'd hold me, every hollow in my being would fill, I'd believe that love was eternal and that every broken thing could be mended. And then she'd leave again, reminding me that every mended thing could also be broken.

I shook my head, meaning only that nothing came after the single syllable of her name.

"I know," she said.

"Well I sure as hell don't."

Her lips drew out thin and pained and she tipped her head to one side as if I'd knocked our world askew and she was trying to right the angle.

"So what were you going to tell me, and could we limit it to the literal truth this time?"

I caught a glimpse of her looking old and almost too tired for pretense.

"The truth? The boring, pointless truth? Nothing. I wanted to sit down with my daughter for a while because I love her, and because someone we both loved is dead. I figured something would come to me."

"Oh, for fuck's sake."

"You wanted the truth. Don't complain if you don't like it."

One way or another, I always got lost in the maze when I talked to Zanne, and I wouldn't get out till I found the door marked LEGITIMATE COMPLAINT, which she'd painted over. I rested my forehead in my hands, as if that would help.

"What if I tell you about your father, then?"

"If it's the truth this time. And if you remember it."

"Oh, I remember it."

She left a pause, then sighed. Truth by its nature was bare and disappointing.

"He was just some guy, sweetheart. By the time I knew I was pregnant, I couldn't remember his name. We'd played a dozen different towns by then, and even if I'd wanted to look for him—"

She righted her head and I could have dropped a plumb line down her spine. Any minute, she'd pull breath into her lungs and sing.

"Besides, I didn't want to share you. I was past the age where I was thinking about having kids and suddenly there you were, blazing away inside me. I was so in love with you."

She was singing, only without the notes. The ballad of the loving mother, and she was younger than she'd been a minute before. The age I'd caught sight of might as well have been a costume she'd put aside so she could step forth with the spark of my life cupped in her hands. The older woman I'd glimpsed hadn't been the real Zanne after all.

There was no real Zanne, just layer after layer of costume and myth.

"I wanted to keep you all to myself."

"Yeah, that worked out well."

"You can't know that ahead of time. I loved you. I thought I could make it work. And believe me, I did try. Anyway, as fathers go, he wasn't promising. Whatever you think I cheated you out of, he didn't have it."

I stared out the window at the winter-locked ground and the picket fence we should have painted while Josie was alive,

46

only it hadn't occurred to me till now. It all looked bleak and unloved, although it wasn't.

I turned back to Zanne.

"So tell me about him."

"There's not much to tell."

I expected this to be a beginning – there's not much to tell and then she'd talk for an hour – but limiting herself to the facts undercut her style. Truth only interested her as a starting point.

If it was the truth. How would I know?

"Do you even know who he was?"

"There weren't that many, sweetheart. It's the men who collect groupies."

"So tell me what you do know."

"He was young. A nice enough guy, in a cowboy-hat-and-beer sort of way. He drank Bud. We were out west somewhere."

"Where out west?"

"*I* don't remember."

She made it sound as if someone else should. Me, maybe. Why wasn't I paying attention?

"It's all a blur between Chicago and California. We were doing a few gigs on the way, and he worked at one of the venues. His name was Earl."

"You said you didn't remember his name."

She tipped her head and the complaint ran off like rain.

"I *think* it was Earl."

"Did he have a last name?"

"I'm sure he did. I didn't happen to hear it and I didn't ask for ID."

If she'd known his full name, would I have looked for him? I didn't feel driven in that direction anymore. When I was a kid, she made up so many different fathers that I gave up and created my own: He was off in the mountains with Che, even if Che was dead. Why should that change anything? I'd join my father when I got big enough, and he'd know me because I'd remind him of a woman he'd always loved. He'd teach me to shoot and we'd fight the revolution together. That was the father who watched me grow up, and I kept him with me well past the age when I should have shaken off that sort of nonsense. Now I imagined a rodeo rider, then replaced him with someone young enough to still have his teenage skinniness. He was too young still to be sure who he was and too taken by his good luck to care that Zanne was twice his age.

If it had been anyone but Zanne and as long as he was old enough to buy his own beer, I wouldn't have cared about the age difference, but I wanted my father to have been all the way into adulthood when he performed his only significant act in my life.

Earl.

Or Not-Earl.

The entire world is divided into people who are named Earl and people who are not named Earl.

I spent a moment staring into the blank surface of my coffee. The words *I don't want to know any more* scrolled across my mind. An excess information warning.

"He had a beautiful head of hair, I remember that. Thick. Black. He could've been part Native American. You have his hair, only wavier."

If she'd told me this when I was a kid, I'd have wished my hair two shades darker, because however much my hair might be like his, it wasn't black. I'd have imagined meeting him at the siege of Wounded Knee and turned myself into some embarrassing, synthetic Indian. Now, though, I couldn't think why a few stray bits of DNA should mean anything. Growing up without the culture, the stolen land, the stolen language, the stolen families, without a hint of what it means to actually be Native, why should some random dip into the gene pool make a difference?

Besides, she was guessing. Or making it up. Half my heritage was imaginary, and if I hadn't grown up with Josie and Sol she'd have invented that half too.

"He wore a heavy ring. Not a wedding ring; other hand. Not that it matters."

The ring and the hair made him older, for some reason, and heavier.

"It's not much of a tale."

"I didn't want a tale."

"No, I don't suppose you did."

It sounded like a failing, the way she said it.

"I should get back to work."

"I suppose you should."

Another failing. Not that she didn't understand work – she worked harder than most people I knew – but the borderline normality of what I did, the sheer day-to-dayness of it, was enough to send her back out on the road, looking for her own version of that cold, open field.

I waited for her to slug down the last of her coffee and go, but I'd confused her with a normal person.

"You could give yourself a day off," she said. "Josie's only just died."

"My deadlines aren't impressed."

The women's shelter deadline was near enough that I wasn't completely lying, and even without it some deadline was always close enough for me to reach out and grab a fistful of pressure. In a perverse sort of way, they kept my life in order.

"You go ahead, then. I'm working on a song for the memorial and I can feel Josie's presence here."

"Josie's gone, Zanne." *Old Josie's dead and gone, left me here to write this song.* "She's not present anywhere. That's one of the ways you can tell someone's dead."

"You do your work and I'll do mine, okay?"

"No, it's not okay. I can't do my work when you're here."

My voice had gone thready and high. If I'd kept talking, my momentum would've carried me past words and into babble.

I shut myself up and breathed in, hoping that when I breathed out I'd exhale youth and powerlessness and the tangles of being Zanne's daughter.

I started over.

"I'm behind schedule and I need to work. You'll have to find her presence someplace else."

The voice that came out of me on that second try was a gift from Josie as surely as if she'd left it to me in her will. It expected to be listened to and it made Zanne stand, leaving the last of her coffee in the cup.

5

I WAS five when I came to live with Josie and Sol.

Sometime before that – I couldn't measure time at that age any more effectively than I could measure air – Zanne told the band she was settling down, she had the kid to think about. In my memory, our apartment was in Iowa City, although Sol swore it was Chicago and Josie, toward the end, thought it might've been in Wisconsin somewhere.

"We never knew where she was, or for how long," she said.

I took this to mean that they watched over me, or tried to. That they were as helpless as I was.

Whatever the city was, I trailed Zanne up a staircase to the apartment. Narrow stairs, narrow window on the landing, a mustard-yellow wall that brushed my shoulder. With one hand I bumped a bag up the stairs and with my free hand clutched the hem of Zanne's jacket.

"We'll have a real home," Zanne was saying. "Just you and me and nobody else. Where we don't share the bathroom with anyone. And you'll ride the school bus."

Some part of me knew better than to get caught up in this, but I couldn't help myself. Zanne carried such power in her voice, even when she was only talking. We'd wake up in the same place, morning after morning, and the same birds would sing outside the same window. The sun would pour in. We'd be happier than any mother and daughter had ever been in the history of humankind.

Zanne unlocked the door and carried the first of our boxes into bare rooms. I hadn't understood that apartments started out empty.

"Zanne, where do we sleep?"

"A friend's bringing a bed over."

Zanne had friends everywhere. They brought beds, gave me candy, called me Summertime, and went away before I needed to lock their names into my memory.

We carried in clothes, Zanne's keyboard and guitar, my toys, the air mattress I slept on backstage or sometimes in an office. I wouldn't need it anymore, but we were still keeping it. You could never tell—

She spread a scarf over an empty box.

"There. That's our dining room table. Are we elegant or what?"

We were elegant. Zanne could make a home out of a scarf and a cardboard box. She knelt down and nuzzled my neck.

"We're home, sweetheart. It's just you and me."

With the sense that I was letting go of a branch and trusting myself to the flood, I let myself believe her.

On my first day of school, I learned that the other kids already knew each other and that they played games with rules no one bothered to explain, although they were quick enough to tell me when I broke one. I learned that the school bus was just a bus. If you got out of your seat, you got yelled

52

at. And when you stayed in it, the other kids said things to you. Or they pretended you weren't there.

Zanne was waiting for me when I got off and we crossed the street to the secondhand store, carrying home a lamp to set beside the bed, a satin spread, a cup with kittens on it, a plastic toy that was too young for me but I'd never had a toy that played music – it might have ended up backstage – so I felt I had a right to it. We walked home happy with each other, and the sun was shining and I was wearing a new jacket and Zanne told me she was going to give lessons. She'd made some contacts while I was in school, and contacts were everything. She'd do local gigs. She didn't have to run around chasing fame, it was enough to be known, and I would grow up free and happy and gorgeous.

This was the beat that drove our lives. Something wonderful was coming. Something wonderful was already here if I could only learn to see it. Our lives were unbounded and full of possibility.

Over the next weeks, we made our way through the secondhand stores: the Goodwill, the Sally, the dented and damaged, the unloved and abandoned, gathering pots, dishes, doilies, embroidered towels too small for a cat, thick towels big enough to wrap around me and still have a bit left to throw over my head. A coffee table. A footstool for the chair we didn't have yet. A TV set with a screen no bigger than my face. Bright-colored scraps and castoffs that we burrowed into like nesting mice. And then, triumphantly, a couch.

The weather turned cold and we lit the space heater, a square metal dragon with a flame inside that terrified me, and we moved the bed into the center room because the bedroom was icy.

The next thing I remember, we were packing everything into bags and boxes and loading it into the car, throwing our bright-colored scraps of cloth into the bin for one of the stores to sell thirdhand, and Zanne was using that voice again. We were going to see Josie and Sol, who loved me *so* much, and I'd sleep toasty warm in the room upstairs, under the roof, where Zanne and Caro had slept when they were little, and I'd dream myself to magical places where girls could fly and butterflies could talk.

I turned my head to watch our apartment disappear. I was suspended in some empty space between happiness and unhappiness, where I felt neither, just watched with minute attention while my life changed. The flood of Zanne's tale wasn't as strong this time, and I kept the branch clutched in my hand while the water pulled at me.

At Josie and Sol's, the chair that had once been by the door still stood by the door, and the same pieces of heavy, hemmed fabric covered the worn spots on its arms. The couch Zanne had bought us, which had looked so big and serious in our apartment, was made of matchsticks compared to Josie and Sol's. If you owned a couch like this, you stayed put, because you couldn't just ask a friend to carry it out the front door. I didn't ask myself how they'd gotten it in. It might as well have been made where it stood, or the house built around it.

We stopped inside the door and I hung onto Zanne's coat. I liked it better when she wore her jacket and I could hold the hem, but I got a grip on her pocket and leaned into her. It wasn't that I didn't know these people – they were Josie and Sol and they were my grandparents – but I wasn't sure what that meant to me. I kept my grip on Zanne's pocket while Sol and Zanne hugged.

"Let me turn this thing off," Josie said, putting an end to the evening news. "It's gotten to be a habit. It's horrible – so openly biased. Can you stay a while?"

"If it's okay."

I'd never heard Zanne say that before. We stayed at people's houses all the time. It was always okay.

"Of course it's okay. You know it's okay."

"Good. Great. I'm just saying."

Sol let out a breath as if he was tired of it and thought the next one might be better.

"Summer, let's go find the toy box while these two talk. You remember where it is?"

No one had told me what to do with my jacket, so I left it on and led Sol upstairs. He didn't tell me I'd find anything wonderful in the box and I liked him for that. He was wide and solid and quiet, and I felt his gentleness in the wordless way a plant feels sun. At the top of the stairs, I took his hand.

"I wasn't sure you'd remember," he said. "It was so long ago, the last time you were here."

"Was I a baby?"

"Not a baby, just younger than you are now."

I tried to remember myself in this house, not a baby but younger than I was now, and came up with the texture of the toy box lid – the gloss of blue paint under my fingers – and a clay dog that whistled when I blew through its tail. The couch and chair downstairs.

"Do I remember being a baby?"

"I don't think so. People don't, really."

"Who took care of me when I was a baby?"

"Zanne did."

"But who took care of me when Zanne was singing?"

"I don't know, sweetheart. She probably found a babysitter."

"I don't think so."

Having a gap in my memory was unsettling, as if the pieces I didn't remember might rattle loose and break something, but I didn't know what question would let me fill it in.

Downstairs, Josie and Zanne's voices were low and snappish, but we'd be on the road again in a few days, so it was okay.

I heard them again that night, through the air vent in the floor, Zanne and Josie's voices taut, Sol's low and steady, like a cartoon boulder speaking.

I woke to Zanne's hand stroking my forehead.

"You awake?"

"Kind of."

"Well, wake up a minute, because I need to tell you something. Can you do that for me?"

I sat up, pulled the blankets around me.

"You know I love you, right?"

I nodded.

"And I think about you every minute of every day?"

The waters were pulling at me.

"Now tell me you'll remember that."

"I'll remember."

"You'll never forget?"

I shook my head.

"You're the best kid anybody ever had. You remember that too."

Zanne choked on the words and she hugged me, and I'd have hugged her back but my arms were trapped inside the blankets.

"Now go to sleep. I'm going to sit up for a while."

In the morning she was gone, along with everything we'd carried in from the car except my suitcase and my box of toys.

Josie came out of the kitchen, her hair loose and her mouth unlipsticked.

"Where's my mommy?"

The question was a measure of how scared I was. I didn't call her Mommy. She was Zanne, the same as I was Summer, Josie was Josie and Sol was Sol.

Josie knelt down to my level, leaning a hand – and it's only now that I understand this – on the armchair to take the weight off her knees.

"I don't know exactly. On the road. She wants you to stay with us so you can go to school."

"I went to school."

Even to me, the words didn't make sense, but I choked on them all the same. Anything closer to what I meant lay beyond speech. It could only be said in wails, but I didn't howl that I wanted my mommy. I understood that she was gone, leaving a Zanne-sized chasm in my life. And I didn't cry. I remember that because I was young enough to think not crying might help. Josie and I balanced there, measuring each other, although I had no idea what I was measuring until I'd decided: the only safety in the world lay with her and Sol.

She sang me to sleep that night, and her voice was off-key and cracked on the high notes, but that only meant it had nothing to do with making strangers love her. She was singing for me alone, and it was more beautiful than any song Zanne had ever sung me.

In my memory of the time before Zanne rented that apartment, I never woke up in the same place two days running. That can't be true – no one's on the road all the time – but it's how I remember our life: I never woke up knowing where the bathroom was, or who I'd find in the kitchen. Sometimes a woman made me breakfast and asked me questions and showed me how to stick glitter to the drawings we made. Sometimes a man sat at the table in his underwear, noodling around on a guitar, and he'd look up long enough to say, "Hey, kid," then look away and keep playing. I remember that as if it happened more than once, although the memory's too specific for that to be possible.

In my memory, I never woke up where I went to sleep. Zanne pumped up my mattress somewhere backstage, and she rolled out my sleeping bag, handed me my bear, whose name was also Zanne, and gave me my sippy cup of magic milk. I was too old for a sippy cup but it was only at night, so we agreed it was okay. I fell asleep listening to her sing and her voice followed me into my dreams so I was never entirely without her. I should be horrified at how casual it all was, but except for the man in his underwear the memories are warm ones. The golden time I imagined we could go back to if only she'd come for me.

One night I followed her voice onto the stage. The bass player shook his head at me, no, and I understood that he meant I shouldn't be there, but it didn't jar loose the thought that I should go back to bed. I *was* there. It was too late to change that.

Zanne stood in the brightest circle of light and sang, held there by the audience's love, and bits of laughter rattled around the hall. At the end of the verse she turned and held a hand out, calling me to her while the band filled the time until she came back in. I was wearing pajamas with feet, clutching Zanne-the-Bear in one arm, and someone in the audience breathed out an involuntary *ohhh*, a downward slide of notes, and I understood what it was to have strangers love me. I took Zanne's hand and surveyed the audience with imperial calm while she finished the song.

During the applause, Zanne-the-Mother lifted me and Zanne-the-Bear to one hip, and when it stopped she sang a song to me and the audience both, about a frog who found an old boot, and inside the boot he found everything he'd ever wanted, but once he held the things in his hands none of them mattered and he threw them away. The audience and I sang with her on the chorus and the band came in behind us, picking it up after a few lines, and we all twined around each other in the music. No child was ever the target of so much love, and it was love that the frog found at the bottom of the boot, which turned out to be what he'd wanted all along. The chorus changed and Zanne sang it alone.

Then she announced an intermission, carried me away

from the lights and tucked me and Zanne-the-Bear back into my sleeping bag. She mixed another magic milk and kissed me and told me to sleep tight and not let the bedbugs bite.

My best guess is that the magic in the cup was brandy. I've never liked the taste of alcohol, but the smell of brandy still carries a whiff of nostalgia.

"We'll do this every night," I said.

That might have been when she decided it was time to settle down.

Josie was in her seventies and still straight-backed and sharp-edged when I came to live with her and Sol. He was older and he'd had a heart attack a few years before, so I walked with him every day – through rain, over icy sidewalks, in the thick heat of summer – and I was sure I was keeping him alive.

It's not impossible that for a while I did.

"Zanne lied to me," I told him once.

I don't remember what lie I was talking about. There were so many.

"She lies to herself."

Whatever I'd expected him to say, that wasn't it, and his answer stayed with me. I'd turn it one way and another, wondering how you lied to yourself. Wouldn't you know?

For years, I listened to Zanne's voice on the tapes and CDs Josie and Sol had. If she sang about love, she was singing for me. If she sang about reunion, that was for me too. If the sun warmed her face, that was me, Summer, sending my love. She'd started out with a folk-rock sound, but after she left the band she never had more than one or two musicians behind her and her voice grew softer and somehow more powerful, as if the sadness of leaving me had poured itself into the music.

Or that's how I read it. For all I know of her, the sadness came from losing whatever momentum she'd had with the band. Or it wasn't sadness at all, just an older voice.

Then I hid the tapes and CDs behind Josie and Sol's books and they pretended not to notice. If they'd given me no other reason to love them, that would have been enough.

Josie went on singing me to sleep until I got too old for it, and the songs that connected us best were the political ones. Every night, the poor fought to feed their families, free their nations, reclaim their dignity. The lady left her husband's goose-feather bed and slept in a field while I ran my fingers over the satin binding Josie stitched back onto my blanket every time it came loose, and I managed not to notice any contradiction.

Was that where I picked up the urge to romanticize the struggle? Or did the songs only reinforce a habit I'd gotten somewhere else? Zanne romanticized, always. The whole damn culture romanticizes. Breathe the air and the impulse will settle in your lungs and reproduce. Don't we all want something to give us meaning? Gods. Heroes. The wondrous fields where all our friends their vigils keep. Life may be shit, but one day beauty will split open this too-tight skin and we'll beat our wings and fly.

At some point after Sol died, when his absence was leaning particularly hard on me, I found Josie in the kitchen and started a song, getting through the first line on my own –

We must never lose our courage in the fight

before she turned away from the carrots and sang with me, vegetable peeler hanging loose in one hand.

Though skies of lead turn days of sunshine into night.
Because the hour for which we yearn will yet arrive,
And our marching step will thunder, we survive.
Because the hour for which we yearn will yet arrive,
And our marching step will thunder, we survive.

I had a half-formed sense that I was doing something dishonest, but she hugged me long and hard and I shoved the possibility aside. Even now, though, it circles back like a fly that won't stop landing on me. As far as I can figure it out, what bothers me is partly that I was using politics to get myself a hug and partly that I was singing the words she'd taught me instead of the rewritten version I sang in the privacy of my head, which shifted *will* to *may* so the hour was no more than possible. Because where was the struggle's heroism if you knew you'd win?

Which was as much as I knew about heroism. Or victory and defeat. Or humans, for that matter. I was ten, maybe eleven years old, a kid with satin binding on her blanket, even if it was weary where I'd rubbed it too often, singing the desperation of the Warsaw Ghetto because she wanted Josie to set aside the carrots and hug her.

I don't know if that's moving or ridiculous or a bit of each. What I do know is that we sang her version: The hour would arrive, like some storm-blown dove finally able to rest.

I'm still waiting.

6

O N the second evening after Josie's death, I didn't call
to tell Shar I missed her, although I did miss her, and
I didn't go to the house to be with her. My phone rang and
I let it roll into voicemail while I drifted through Josie's home,
ghostlike, there and not there. I touched the spines of books,
touched the shelves Sol had built – every ten years, they
needed a new set, he told me once, and I took that as a goal:
this was how much a person should read. My hand brushed
past trade union history, the Spanish Civil War, a biography
of Lincoln, two of Mandela, volume one of Marx's *Capital*. I'd
plowed my way through its endless first chapter before I gave
up. All I took away was that it had something to do with an
ell of cloth. Whatever an ell was, it didn't matter enough to
look it up – it was a length; what more did I need to know? –
but it bothered me that the word was so obscure. This was the
mighty Marx? An ell of cloth?

On the other side of the couch, they'd shelved the Red
Scare, the trial of Ethel and Julius Rosenberg, educational
theory, more educational theory, fiction, children's books
left from when Caro, Zanne and Jack were kids, and, mixed

in with them, like markers of my passage through their lives, the ones I'd added.

I pulled down a few of the political books, not reading anything, just holding them, as if Josie and Sol's certainty would seep through the covers and into my hands: their belief that the human race moved forward, that the river of history would deposit us, exhausted and triumphant, on the shores of a socialist state, where we'd build a society fit to live in. If I'd lived in the thirties or forties knowing where it all went – Stalin, Mao, Pol Pot, the corruption inherent in one-party rule – I don't see how I could have been a Communist, and I'd have missed out on everything that gave Josie and Sol their generosity and their strength.

Marx was big on contradictions, I understood that much, and I can find a fair few in our lives, although I doubt they're the kind he had in mind.

A memory came back to me – nothing to do with books or politics: the morning after one of Josie's later strokes, I crept into her bedroom at eight thirty and put a hand on her shoulder. It was some half an hour after she usually got up. Her shoulder was tiny by then, the bone barely cushioned by flesh, the skin a thin drape on top of them both. She slept on.

"Josie?"

She didn't roll over, just asked, "Is it morning?"

When I was little, she woke up as sharply as a guard dog. Now her voice was claggy with sleep. The stroke had changed her sleep patterns, her thought patterns, her self patterns, until she was someone I didn't quite know. I wondered whether, in a decent world – as she would have put it back when words were simple – there might not have been a way to bring more of her back to us. But death comes to us all, and sometimes it comes in pieces. Reorganize the world in whatever way we can, we still die, and mostly not the way we want.

I couldn't help wondering, though. I'm Josie's grand-daughter. I'll always half believe there's a better way, a better world, already formed and waiting for us to break down the door and step through.

"It's past eight," I said.

"Can't I sleep?"

As if it was up to me.

It was up to me.

"I'll call you later."

Two hours later, I stood by the door until I knew she was breathing, then woke her a second time.

"Can't I sleep?" she asked again.

"You'll be up all night."

And I'd be up all night, because if I went to bed and she fell again, I wouldn't know about it till morning.

"An hour. I'll get up in an hour."

Half the night, then.

I went back to the computer, calculating how much of my working day was going to disappear into the small moments of waking and washing and eating and trailing behind Josie's walker. More than last week but not yet all of them. I could do this. I could still do it. Then the flow of work took over and I stopped thinking.

At eleven thirty I woke her a third time and she took hold of her walker and raised herself, each muscle needing a separate Central Committee directive, and I trailed her to the bathroom, one arm hovering in case her legs gave out, although I wasn't sure I could break her fall if they did.

At the toilet, she turned, a set of shuffling steps I wasn't used to, then stopped, the walker in front, the grab bars behind, and twisted around to look.

"Reach your hand back."

I guided one hand, then the other.

"Can I get your nightgown?"

What I'd wanted to ask was whether I could lift her nightgown, but *lift* was too real a word for me. I gathered, I lifted, and I put my free hand on Josie's back to steady her while she lowered herself, then stood outside the open door, pretending I wasn't listening to my grandmother pee. I felt an odd combination of necessary and useless.

The toilet flushed and I went back in, hovering while Josie cleaned her teeth, put in her bridge, brushed her hair, all in slow, meticulous motions.

She pointed.

"The thing with the water."

"The bath?"

"The other thing."

"The shower."

"The shower. I'll do it tomorrow."

She smelled stale and old, but only when I stood close by. Add a layer of clothes and she'd be fine.

It was just the two of us anyway.

She worked her way, muscle by muscle, into the clothes I set out, although I had to hook the bra across the slack flesh of her back. It was oddly matter-of-fact, dressing her.

66

This is a body. This is how you put clothes on it. As if I was thinking about someone else, I remembered the undertow of embarrassment I'd felt as a kid at how naked my dolls were under their clothes.

If only I could manage that same detachment from the rest of my childhood.

I poured Josie's coffee, buttered her toast, set jam on the table.

"I don't want," Josie said, and reached the limit of the words she'd called up.

"Toast? Coffee?"

"Not that. You."

Another pause. She hadn't hurt my feelings, although in an abstract sort of way I could see where she might have.

She turned in her chair, pointed.

"I can't find the word."

"Upstairs?"

"Not that."

I poured my own coffee and sat in my spot, not quite across from her.

"Eat your toast. It'll come to you."

I didn't know that it would, and wished I could unmake my promise. Josie always took her truths head-on, however unlikable they were.

She picked up the spoon and worked it around in the jar, then stopped. The days when she could catch jam with a spoon and talk at the same time were gone.

"Work," she said. "Go back to work."

Her voice had gone flat, laying the same weight on each word.

"You'll be okay?"

"I'll be okay."

It was like an exercise from some off-kilter language class. You will be okay? I will be okay. He, she, it will be okay. We will all be okay. She was fighting to link her thoughts to words so she could send them into the world. It was pure Josie, fighting her way back as best she could until the next stroke – and I didn't kid myself about whether there'd be one – swept her gains away. And it was pure Josie to send me back to work so I wouldn't lose my whole day to her. She was still in there, struggling to take care of me. I kissed her cheek and she reached a hand up to cup one side of my jaw, as if even now she wanted to protect me.

We'd said "I love you" often enough, but the words were nothing. All that mattered was this one raw gesture.

7

IN the morning, I was supposed to meet Claudette at TOCK-the-K-is-silent but I lost track not so much of time as of myself, lying on Josie's couch, staring at the walls, feeling my way toward the idea of moving back in with Shar, Tee and Zac. I saw Tee folding her laundry on the floor, Shar warming soup I couldn't eat, Zac miming the recoil of his imaginary rifle, Josie saying it would take more than the Occupy camp to make a revolution.

Which for no good reason drove me back to reality, and to an understanding that time still passed. I hauled myself off the couch and got to TOCK late. Claudette was outside her office, standing next to a weeping mother, a small woman with one hand holding a purse and the other the wall, as if she needed its support.

"They say he has to have the pills or he can't come to school. But he's got these circles." The mother's hand left the wall to draw half-moons under her eyes. "He can't sleep."

Claudette gestured an apology at me and guided the woman into her office, leaving me in what passed for a waiting room, the chair-lined hallway of a church basement. I set my computer bag at my feet and leaned the back of my head uncomfortably against the wall.

When I was a kid, I used to sit here, or sometimes in the office, with coloring books, picture books, schoolwork – a variation, now I think of it, on the time I spent backstage while Zanne sang. My measure of adulthood was to be a tutor here. I'd teach kids how to read and know they'd have been lost without me. I might as well have imagined myself as a missionary. Summer Dawidowitz, angel of the left, saving little children from the jaws of illiteracy.

By the time I was old enough to be a tutor, I'd lost interest. TOCK was too small, too polite, too much like social work. I was going to be purer, further left and way more exciting than Josie. I went to the Seattle anti-World Trade Organization demonstrations, and the talk there wasn't about socialism but about anti-capitalism. We were going to change everything. No one I met had a clear idea of what we'd change it into, but I didn't notice at the time. We seemed to be everywhere, and I felt—

Oh hell, I felt like Zac must've when he said the Occupy movement was the revolution. Then everyone went home, the whole thing disappeared, and I couldn't figure out what we'd accomplished.

I never said, "Josie, I don't think things are going to change. I think the bad guys are going to be in charge forever." It wasn't the kind of thing you said to Josie. At least it wasn't the kind of thing I said to her, and I didn't have the words for it anyway. It was more a feeling, a weight, than a coherent thought. In hindsight, I wish I had said it so I'd know how she'd have answered.

Claudette's door opened and the mother walked past without letting her eyes pick me out from the row of plastic chairs. No one but Claudette had seen her cry. She clutched a sheaf of papers – on hyperactivity, I guessed, on Ritalin, on Adderall, on how to challenge school decisions, on how to join TOCK and advocate for her child.

I knocked at Claudette's open door, apologized for interrupting, apologized for being late.

"Not your fault. I'd have asked her to come back on parents' night, but she's in bad shape. And she doesn't have a car."

She shook her head, giving the woman's troubles a moment's recognition and then a sigh. "Never mind her, tell me about you. How're you doing?"

"Oh, you know."

"Don't I just."

She hadn't said anything six other people couldn't have, but something about the way Claudette listened made you feel you could tell her anything – or tell her nothing, as I had, and be understood in spite of it. I couldn't know how deep that went – we worked together without being friends in any personal way – but I didn't need to. It was warmth and I was grateful for it.

And Josie had trusted her. She thought Claudette leaned more toward social work than organizing, but that had as much to do with the changing times as it did with her individually.

"Come in. Close the door and let's get this done."

This: figuring out what to do about the hole that had appeared in TOCK's budget. Claudette was hopeless with numbers, but even she could see what was coming. TOCK had been founded with guilt money from Josie's brother, the same David Freund who Caro had wanted to include in the obit. Every month he'd sent Josie more money than she would have earned as a teacher, and she passed it on to TOCK. Before she was old enough to draw Social Security, it paid her a salary, leaving her at least technically innocent of taking his money, and what was left over went into TOCK's account. Or if you wanted to look at it the other way – and Josie would have – it paid Claudette's salary and TOCK paid Josie's.

I'd never been sure what David Freund was guilty of, but with Josie's death, we were pretty sure his guilt was expunged, so we were about to lose our biggest source of income.

We talked about fundraising events we could hold, grants we could apply for, individuals we could approach, crowdfunding gimmicks we could try. We talked short-term patches and long-term solutions. We talked about what the organization would have to cut to save that much and all the reasons it might not survive if it did. TOCK had a crisis fund, but it was the size of a small, well-behaved crisis, not the kind that broke down doors and threw things.

"What about Esther?" Claudette said.

Esther was a donor. Not on David Freund's scale, but on the scale of leftish organizations, a big one.

"Her husband's dying. I haven't been sure it's okay to call."

"I knew he'd been ill, but— Oh, lord. I'll send a note."

A short pause while we ran other possibilities through our heads.

"I could talk to David Freund. I can't imagine it'll help, but we should give it a try."

"You sure you want to do that?"

"When did what I want come into it?"

"I can't tell you it wouldn't be a good idea, but that money tore Josie apart. You know it did."

I wouldn't have put it that way, but now that I'd heard the words, yes, it had.

"He's not my brother. That should make some sort of difference."

"Let's put him at the bottom of the list. He's not our best shot anyway."

"She ever tell you what happened between them?"

"I never asked."

She separated the words, making it sound like asking would have set off an IED.

"I did. You know what I was like as a kid. I couldn't let it go. All she'd tell me was, 'He knows and I know, and that's more than enough.'"

"I do miss that woman."

We nodded a kind of memorial, then ran through likelier donors – people who might find a few thousand dollars in loose change if they looked under the couch cushions. We talked about a loan: Where we could get one. How we could pay it back. *If* we could pay it back. We planned a fundraiser that would double as a tribute to Josie. We speculated about how much people would contribute in her memory, but neither of us had anything to base our guesses on so the numbers were imaginary. By the time I left, we had something that looked like a plan, although it was mostly spun sugar and good wishes.

Back at Josie's, I called the donors we'd agreed on, asking if I could come by and talk. One said he was at his limit. A second agreed to meet, and if we'd known ten of her we could have plugged the hole, but we didn't. The third had enough spare change to cover Greece's budget deficit, never mind TOCK's, but she was a member of that rare species, the massively rich super-radical, and TOCK wasn't radical enough to set her brain cells dancing. Or her hormones. Or whatever it was that drove her. The last time I'd approached her, she told me that by tutoring kids TOCK was taking pressure off the schools – they didn't have to teach their hard-to-reach students because TOCK would. I didn't remind her that TOCK wasn't big enough to take pressure off the schools. Instead I argued that the tutoring programs drew parents to the organization and once they were there TOCK taught them to advocate for the kids themselves, which was a deeply radical thing to do. They took power into their own hands. And TOCK could coordinate that pressure when it saw a pattern of failure, which pressured the schools more effectively than leaving kids to flounder.

All power to the parents.

We were sitting in her living room, looking through floor-to-ceiling glass at the lake where the city's robber barons had built their mansions in the nineteenth century. They'd have run their lawns down to the water and kept the riffraff out of sight if the shoreline hadn't been turned into a park. The name of the commissioner who'd pulled off that magic trick was engraved on the memory of every good Minneapolis leftist except mine. I looked at the wind-ruffled water, sipped pale green tea from an even paler green Japanese cup, and scrabbled for his name in the blank spot where I'd expected to find it.

"TOCK is doing the most revolutionary thing possible in nonrevolutionary times," I told her, with a dizzying sense of unreality, "and that's organizing ordinary people to defend their interests."

I wondered if I should have said *working-class people*. Or *poor people*. That was one of the problems of being politically multilingual. I was never sure how to divide and label the world's population for any given audience.

Theodore Wirth. The park commissioner was Theodore Wirth.

I got a small – for her – onetime donation, probably for using the word *revolutionary*. It was a measure of my desperation that I was calling her again, but she agreed to meet.

Josie never wanted TOCK to depend on the whims of the rich. Build a broad base, she argued. Rely on the people whose kids TOCK tutors, and on the people who volunteer for TOCK, and on their friends, their relatives, their neighbors. Build a network. Organize, organize, organize. But the days of seventy-five-dollar rents were gone, and it takes a hell of a lot of ten-dollar donations to buy a single computer, never mind cover salaries and health insurance and books and paper and pens and calculators. Even hundred-dollar donations mount up too slowly. And since the organization was already dependent on the whims of David Freund, she was in no position to push too hard. So on TOCK's behalf, I courted the wealthy and was grateful we had a few to court.

Caro and Steve weren't full-blown wealthy, just affluent – you have to hang around money to see the line between those categories – but they'd make a donation, out of sentiment if not commitment. Jack and Raymond weren't affluent, they were comfortable, but they'd give more than Caro and Steve.

If Zanne had any money, she'd give it, but money never stayed with her long. That made it a matter of timing. What she would do was sing at a fundraiser, and that would bring in something. Not enough, but something.

On calculations such as this, the organization tottered.

I was between calls when Shar reached me on the landline. She wanted me to spend the night at the house. Everybody would be home. Everybody missed me.

A single night wasn't much to ask for and I told her I couldn't.

"What if I come over there?"

Some dam broke and yes, I wanted that. As badly as if it was the only thing I did want.

An hour later we were sitting on the living room floor, eating Vietnamese food from the cartons she'd brought it in, reproducing the way we'd sat as kids. We could have set up my Barbies on the floor between us if Josie'd saved those mistreated hunks of hair and plastic. Which she might well have. I hadn't looked.

At the start of our friendship, my Barbies were at least as much of an attraction for Shar as I was. Her parents didn't allow them in the house. They'd distort her body image as surely as refined sugar would make her hyperactive and synthetic fabrics would leach volatile organic chemicals into her bloodstream. I never found out what tap water would do, but they had spring water delivered in five-gallon bottles.

At my house, we ranged freely through packaged cookies, giant bags of M&M's, the contents of a miniature gum
machine Caro and Steve had given me, the handful of battered Barbies I'd inherited and hadn't cared about until Shar
came into my life. I never knew if they'd been Zanne's or
Caro's or if they'd each had some.

I asked Shar now if she remembered the Barbies and she
stuck her chopsticks in the box so she could mime shame,
forehead bent to the back of her hand.

"Josie was so much smarter about that than my parents.
If they'd let me have one, in two weeks I wouldn't have given
a shit."

She was sitting Buddha-style across from me and lifted a
piece of tofu with her chopsticks, holding the carton under
her chin to catch imaginary drips as delicately as Barbie herself would if Barbie ate vegetarian Vietnamese food straight
from the carton. One foot rested upside down on her thigh,
where a patch of waffled long-john showed through the
rip in her black jeans. She was the ultimate anti-consumer:
Anarchist Barbie. As an accessory, she carried nothing.

Or not nothing. She had a phone so old it was retro. She
had chopsticks, a cardboard carton of Vietnamese food with
noodles showing at the top, and a student loan the size of
Montana.

I shouldn't make her sound trivial. She was a serious
person, deeply committed to her beliefs, with a degree in
library science that got her fuck all in the way of work and
a job behind the food co-op's deli counter. She'd debated
about grad school but in the end couldn't see the point.
It would only mean more debt and a job behind the food

co-op's deli counter. Besides, I was just as easy to caricature, wearing my flannel shirt and jeans while Fundraiser Barbie's clothes hung in my closet, waiting for me to step into character. I had a laptop in a zippered case as an accessory.

The games of our childhood, still laying down the patterns of our thoughts. Maybe her parents had been onto something.

Shar chased a few final noodles around the base of her carton and set it aside. I'd eaten half of mine and would have asked if she wanted the rest but she'd fuss about whether I was eating enough, so I left it for tomorrow and talked about TOCK, about money, about Jack and Raymond, about Caro and Steve. Not about Zanne. Zanne was a sliver jammed too deep into my fingertip to dig out, and why shouldn't I fold the finger under when I had the luxury? We talked about the memorial no one was ready to plan, the hospital, the fact that people die. I tried to explain how Josie's death had left me with no home in the world.

I listened to myself and thought I shouldn't be saying that to someone who not only loved me but was sitting across the room from me because I wouldn't come to her in the home we'd shared. I could call two separate buildings my home. Talk about luxury. But I couldn't unsay the words or unfeel their truth.

She told me she understood, but she didn't. Her parents were still alive and annoying her with parental regularity. She had no idea how far she was from understanding.

Shar patted the rug beside herself and I slid across, letting the sofa support my back, running the tips of my fingers down the backs of hers. For a while neither of us needed to talk, and then, for whatever reason, she did.

"I respect your process, but we miss you at the house."

I said, "I know," as if that meant something, although it was nothing but mortar to keep the moment that came before tight against the one that followed. The word *process* stuck in my head like a weed in a dog's tail. My process. What the fuck was my process?

That was what was wrong with the Household: words like *process* and all the prefabricated thinking they dragged along with them.

"I need some time, that's all."

She told me again that she understood, and again that they missed me, that *she* missed me, but I'd closed myself off and even if I'd wanted to open back up I wouldn't have known how. *That* was my fucking process.

I drew a long, slow breath and exhaled the anger I was starting to cultivate. *Process* was nothing more than a word. It didn't matter.

It did still matter, but it mattered a hair's breadth less.

"I noticed something on Sunday," I said. "When Zac came in. It seemed like the two of us shifted to the background so he could take over."

I listened to myself the way I might have listened to a stranger. Did the person who said that care or was she only talking to fill a silence? Had she noticed that two of us hadn't shifted to the background but three, because Tee had also been there?

"Did we?"

She slid sideways to look at me and her hand pulled away. This was too serious for distractions. This was *process*. If we were the seeds of a better world, we had to genetically engineer ourselves or we'd reproduce the same damn culture we grew up in.

"Is that something we always do? It wasn't just that once?"

"It felt familiar."

"See? That's another reason we need you back: to tell us stuff like that. We're not whole without you."

A wave of exhaustion broke over me and I leaned the back of my head against the couch, searching for support but instead stretching my neck past what was comfortable. Even so, I kept it there, closed my eyes, and hid for a few moments in the darkness behind my lids.

"Shar, forget it. I shouldn't have brought it up."

"No, this matters."

"Maybe it does, but I can't do it. I can't *discuss* it."

I said "discuss" as if it was a whole different thing than talking. For no good reason, I remembered Zanne offering to repeat "Fuck that" in Latin, and I wished Steve had asked her to.

"You want to talk to him about it, you talk to him. I'm tired."

She said she would but she hadn't noticed it happening. It wouldn't mean as much.

I shrugged as best I could with the couch behind my shoulders and thought about Zac's energy, the way he pulled us in his wake. I thought about Zanne. Then I shut the book of my mind and lost the page. I wasn't going to talk about to Shar about Zanne.

"You're not leaving us, are you?"

I said, "I'm not," but the words were clipped and stingy.

"C'mere then."

She shifted toward me, put an arm around my shoulders, warm and awkward, and I let her pull me in. Our bones met in all the wrong places, and even so it was like rain on dry fields. I rested my head against hers and waited to be lifted by whatever it was that took me the last time we did this, but the wave didn't come and we stayed earthbound. Floorbound. I didn't want to make love, and I felt that absence as its own kind of grief.

After a while we turned on the TV and watched a *Star Trek* rerun – the series where the captain was a woman and didn't fade into the background for anyone, but it was all so painless in whatever the hell century it was set in, when all Earth's problems had been solved and they had to go looking for some in outer space.

During an ad, I asked – casual conversation; nothing important – what was going on with Zac and his guns.

"That was me, actually," she said. "I had this extracurricular activity—"

She nodded to one side, giving a sense of something extending into the distance. That would be the extracurricular activity: someone who wasn't part of the Household but who one of us slept with. Not someone the rest of us had to make space for.

"Sexually it didn't go anywhere – I was missing you or I'd never have thought it would – but she likes to hunt and I went target shooting with her a few times. And it got me thinking, you know?"

I didn't know, and I looked at Shar with a sense that I never had known her – not the real her, the one underneath Anarchist Barbie's outfit. She was a vegetarian, for

81

fuck's sake. I seemed to remember her not being a fan of violence.

I pictured Anarchist Barbie slinging a rifle over her shoulder, and she looked good with it. The accessory every girl's saving up for.

Was I being unfair? People did sometimes change their thinking, even when it was deeper than a layer of makeup.

"It's not like we're starting a militia. It's just – realistically, we can't be the only ones who don't know which end of the gun you point at the enemy."

"Zac seemed—"

I ran out of words and she said, "He's enthusiastic—"

It was her turn to look for words.

"It's new still. He'll settle into it."

I nodded, not because I thought he would necessarily – there'd been a charge in the way he talked about the gun range that didn't bring settling to mind – but because ordinary politeness demanded it. We were sitting on Josie's floor, ignoring *Star Trek*, which had started up again, and we were talking, for all that we hadn't said so, about shooting people. Because that's what you do when guns meet politics. And unless fate is improbably kind, it's what you do in a revolution. It was the part of being in the mountains with Che that I never imagined. I saw myself holding a gun, shooting a gun, letting the gun's power flow through me, but in the safety of my head no one bled. No one felt pain. No one died.

"Who *are* you?" I asked Shar. Not because I meant to but because it was the question my mind formed and because it fell out of my mouth.

She laughed. As if being someone I didn't recognize was a joke to both of us.

When Shar and I first got together, she, Zac and Tee were in the talking stage of forming a family. It was Thanksgiving Day, we hadn't seen each other in years, and she was crossing the street from the bus stop to her parents' house as I parked to pick Josie up and drive her to Caro and Steve's. Thanksgiving there was inescapable – our family merged, oil-and-vinegar style, with Steve's, over stiff conversation and starched napkins at the dining room table. Christmas was at Jack and Raymond's, with plates balanced on our laps in the living room and side dishes forgotten in the refrigerator and emerging with the dessert.

The Jewish holidays slipped past us like songs we'd seen on paper but whose music had never lifted off the page.

I called out to Shar before I had time to ask myself if I wanted to. Our friendship had cooled not long after we outgrew the Barbies, on the day she convinced me that we should take our clothes off and see what would happen if we touched each other's nipples. We were at her house and her parents were off doing whatever it was parents did, either in the house or outside somewhere. They might as well have been in another city, leaving us on the floor of her bedroom with the door closed, because they didn't worry about what two girls could get up to.

Her finger was as delicate as mist, and a feeling I had no name for bolted through me. I was sure it wasn't sexual because what I understood about sex was that it involved two people, and even though two of us were present this was so much inside myself that I might as well have been alone.

Poor Josie. She'd done her best to explain sex, but it was like trying to explain food to a creature who didn't eat in its first phase of life.

Shar's finger stayed too long and was gone too soon, and enough sweat poured down my sides that I put my clothes on so they'd absorb it. That seemed important. I was terrified of the power I felt in what we were doing. Of the flood, maybe. Of I don't know what. Any explanation I come up with now is too neat to match the reality. None of my later fumblings in high school matched the intensity of that moment, not only because they involved boys but because they were so predictable – a kiss, a clench, a grab for whatever body part the boy thought was the hallway to heaven.

Shar had unlocked a door I wasn't ready to open again for years.

Our friendship wasn't easy to drop out of, not least because we lived on the same block, but I made sure we never had another chance to see what would happen if we touched the other body parts my mind kept suggesting.

Seeing her on the street that Thanksgiving, though, both of us grown and her wearing a black jacket with the circled anarchist *A* on the back, reminded me of why I'd run away and why I didn't have to anymore. I'd spent the summer and fall working part-time for an organic gardening service while I built up my fundraising business, and I was pared down to bone and muscle. As I walked toward her, I was conscious of my body as much more than the place I lived. It was a creature with its own will, and it wanted to reach toward her, and so we smiled, my body and I, and I told her how glad I was to see her.

Why didn't we get together later, I asked, when we'd shed our families?

We went to my place – where else could we go on Thanksgiving but her place or mine? – and I dug out half a bottle of wine someone had left behind. I don't know what it tasted like. Vinegar, probably. She didn't complain but she didn't drink much either. We traded family news, centering on who'd come to Thanksgiving, who'd offended who and how, and what had been said, not to mention what hadn't been said but was louder than what had been. When we'd worn that out, we moved on to jobs and relationships. I talked about grant-writing and having just broken off with a girlfriend. We hadn't been living together, so I still had my studio apartment, a nice little place the landlords had carved out of their attic. Now that I couldn't expect company in my bed, though, it had gotten lonely.

With Shar sitting on one end of my couch, legs stretched toward me, feet close enough that I could have touched them but hadn't yet, the place came to life again. Enough to make me wonder when I'd last swept the floor or vacuumed the rug, never mind dusted.

I had washed the dishes. That much I kept up with. As long as you fed yourself and washed the dishes, you weren't depressed.

At some point in the evening, she said, "I have to tell you about this thing that's happening in my life. It's wonderful."

What she told me about was Zac, Tee, bisexuality, poly-amory, how happy it made her to be committed and free, both at the same time. I weighed only what that meant for the night, and her hands, when they finally did touch me, were as light as they'd been that first time, and as unexpected, as if I'd never made love with a woman before. As if I'd never known the full range of what my body could feel. I was more naked with her than I'd been in my life.

A week or so later, I met Zac and Tee.

"If we can't learn to love each other," Zac said, "how are we going to build a better world?"

It was too simple a way of thinking and at the same time it was appealing, and I noticed both. He turned love into both the path to a better world and the better world itself. It was the revolution we could make before the economic and political revolution hauled its recalcitrant ass into sight.

Not as deep as he wants to be, I thought.

Naive, I thought.

Even so, I liked him.

Tee struck me as fragile, maybe clingy, someone I'd have been afraid of in a relationship, but I wasn't getting into a relationship with her. If she needed carrying, Zac and Shar could carry her. It would be fine.

Besides, I liked her warmth. I told myself it balanced out the fragility. One of these days I'll remember that if I have to tell myself something, it's probably because I don't believe it.

When I told Josie I was moving in with them I found myself stuck with the words Zac had used: How else were we going to build a better world?

"By organizing," she said.

"No one does that twenty-four hours a day."

She had a way of rocking her head – a slow tilt first to one ear and then to the other – that said she wouldn't argue but didn't agree, and Zac's words took on a thin, tinny sound in my memory. Then she brought her head back to center and said, "You have to choose the way you'll live. Just be sure it's what you want."

"It is."

"Then I won't say, 'In my day, we didn't do it that way.' It's not my day anymore."

8

WHEN Shar left the next morning, I made a few calls, letting people know I was working at full speed again, and hungry, and I started on a grant for an organization serving LGBT teens. They were a difficult group, the Ls, the Ts and the Gs all pulling in different directions. I still hadn't met any Bs and guessed they were theoretically welcome but were off playing in some different sandbox. The only thing that kept everyone together – other than homophobia and the religious right – was suspicion over how many hours it took me to write a simple grant application. The fact that they changed their minds in every email wouldn't have a thing to do with it.

I took revenge by writing them into my deadline book as the gay, bacon, lettuce and tomato group and hoped the words wouldn't find their way out of my mouth someday in a meeting.

When the doorbell rang, I half expected Zac or Tee, or the two of them together, wanting to discuss sexist assumptions or guns or when I was moving back in. Instead I found a stranger, framed by the glass oval set into the front door and looking like a Victorian portrait – the kind of man I could only describe as an elderly gentleman.

Relief flowed through my veins.

"My name is David Freund."

His voice was muffled by the door but not so heavily I couldn't hear him. "I'm looking for the descendants of Josephine Freund" – a quarter-breath of a pause here, as if he hadn't practiced the next word – "Dawidowitz."

My first impulse was to keep him out – hadn't Josie told me not to open the door to strangers? – but this wasn't someone who'd mug me or steal the Freund family silver that Josie used to make jokes about and that he probably inherited. I cracked open the door and, by way of a compromise, set my foot behind it.

"Yes," I said, and it came out half as a statement and half as a question, meaning I wasn't sure what. Yes, you're looking for them. Yes, I am one. Yes, I understand you're David Freund, although you're nothing like what I imagined.

What had I imagined? He'd haunted my dreams when I was a kid, but I couldn't remember having given him a face or a body. He was the disembodied proof that anyone could do you wrong, even if you loved them. Even if they loved you. Even if you had no idea what sort of wrong you were talking about.

It occurred to me for the first time that *anyone can do you wrong* wasn't the lesson Josie meant for me to take from David Freund's story and then that Josie hadn't told me about him so I could learn a lesson. She told me because he existed, and because pretending he didn't would only give him more power.

He smiled and took his hat off with outdated formality.

"I gather, then, that I've found one of them."

I nodded. The words *I'm her granddaughter* scrabbled inside my head, trying to scratch their way out, but not saying them seemed like a way to honor Josie and everything she'd stood for.

"I wonder if I might come in. I've waited a long time to meet you."

I turned my head to look behind me, as if Josie might still be sitting in the living room, saying, *No, close the door, lock this man out of your life.*

Donor, I told the Josie in my head.

She shook her head, no, and her lips formed a tight, flat line of disapproval. Cold air rushed in from the porch. Heat rushed out.

"I don't think that's a good idea."

It came out as a whisper.

"Then perhaps we could get a cup of coffee somewhere."

I hesitated, not so much thinking about the idea as taking refuge in a moment's blankness, and in that blankness my decision made itself.

"Let me get my keys."

When I was a kid, Josie had warned me about letting strangers in but never about going out for coffee with them, and the Josie in my head – the one who advised my adult, grieving self – had gone silent. The advice she'd given me years ago would have to stand, because she was past updating it. I shut the door on him, letting rudeness make what I'd agreed to do feel less like a betrayal, and I grabbed my jacket and shoved a ten and some change into my pocket, along with my keys.

On the porch, with the locked door behind us, we both hesitated.

"Is there someplace nearby? It's not a neighborhood I know anymore."

He'd parked something big and stodgy at the curb. I'd have guessed a Cadillac but I was too far away to know. Maybe I only thought so because I'd turned him into the capitalist from a 1930s cartoon – the Cadillac, the bags of money, the top hat. Whatever make the car was, though, I wasn't about to ride in it with him, and I wasn't going to invite him into mine.

As long as Josie was alive, the simple fact that she pulled air through her lungs had been enough to keep him stoppered in his world and away from ours. Now he was free to pour himself in. It was a new reason to miss her.

"There's a place on Lake Street. Do you mind if we walk?"

"Not at all."

Like Josie until the last year of her life, David Freund walked like someone fifteen years younger than he was, and he had something of Josie in the tilt of his head and the set of his shoulders. He was as eerily close to her as anyone living, and as far from her as it was possible to be.

At the coffee shop, he stepped ahead to open the door and I accepted this. It trapped him at the back of the line, where he couldn't get to the cash register first to pay for my coffee.

The woman at the counter had a pierced lip and a tattoo rising out of her torn neckline. I didn't know her, and that was a measure of how little I'd gotten out lately. Josie and I had been regulars here for a while. I liked the tattoos and piercings, although I didn't have any myself, and the screw-you-if-you-don't-like-it approach to customer service. Not to mention the coffee, which wasn't screw-you. The place wouldn't have been Josie's first choice, but once she got used to it she saw past their style, and for their part they were sweet to her.

I made a gesture from myself to David.

"I'm paying for these."

David opened his mouth to argue, then thanked me instead. *Noblesse oblige*, Josie said inside my head with that quirked half smile she'd once had – the one the first stroke had stolen – and she was right: He was allowing me to pay, but I discovered an odd power in observing that and remaining untouched.

Thank you, I thought to her.

A mixed blessing, she said – she who never believed in blessings but knew how mixed whatever you wanted to call them could be.

David Freund and I ordered coffee with nothing to soften it – no muffins, no frothed milk, no sugar; like Josie, he drank it black – and we sat at the back, in armchairs almost as old as Josie's. That was another thing I liked here, the sense that I was in someone's living room.

"How were you related, then?" David Freund said.

"She raised me."

My voice was flat and kept him from asking for the story, although I swear I felt him marking it down as something to learn about. This was no way to woo a donor, and I told myself that, but I wasn't listening.

"I expect you've heard of me, then."

"She talked about you."

"Then you understand—"

He let the sentence fade away, and this would've been the place to ask what the hell he'd done, but all the grief in my body told me the guilty verdict Josie had passed was as much as I needed to know. Besides, I understood enough: why he had to come, why he'd waited until she was dead, why his gentleness was tinged so heavily with regret. My lips pulled tight at the corners in disapproval. Another of Josie's faces, and one I don't think I'd ever made before I met him. I couldn't find words to either soften it or match it and a silence stretched between us, taut and awkward. My eyes drifted upward and found a focus in a piece of art someone had hung on the wall above his shoulder, an abstract blob of color that resolved into a papier-mâché breast painted a camouflage pattern of green, blue and pink. Through the gloss and paint, I made out newspaper headlines. Above his other shoulder hung its older, droopier cousin, made of prim, daisy-print cotton and shellacked into a solid.

I drew my eyes to the bridge of his glasses and fixed them there. It was the only way I could keep from turning to see what was in his line of sight on the wall behind me.

"I'm sorry," he said. "I don't know your name."

"Summer. Dawidowitz."

"Summer." He weighed the name, giving it more consideration than it could stand up to. "It's a beautiful name."

"I was born," I said, "in November."

He tipped his head to one side in a kind of acknowledgment.

"Even so."

In spite of myself, I laughed. It was an absurd name – the kind of thing Zanne must have wanted for herself. "Even so" was as close as anyone had yet come to balancing tact against an honest reaction, and god damn it, I liked him for it.

"I'm sorry if I seem—" The word *rude* was too bald, and I left a gap where it would have gone. "The thing is, Josie wouldn't have wanted—"

My throat closed off the end of the sentence.

He smiled again, looking even gentler, even more regretful.

"No, I don't suppose she would have. I did try to make things right with her. It's important to me that you know that."

"She wouldn't have felt—"

I couldn't finish that either. Whatever things we were talking about, she'd never felt he could make them right. Any more than – fundraising be damned – I felt I should be drinking coffee with him. I hadn't expected it to be so personal, talking to him.

"I loved Josie very much. I like to think she knew that."

She had, and I refused him the comfort of hearing it. She'd also loved him back, or loved the person he'd once been, or the one she'd thought he was, and I refused him this too. It was a small and pointless tribute, and I clung to it.

"What happened," he said, then let his gaze get lost for long seconds on the surface of his coffee.

I sat suspended, outside of time, then he looked up as if he'd made a decision.

"At the time I thought it would kill me, and I mean that quite literally. I tried it twice but I lacked the – determination,

94

I'd have to say. I don't tell you this to excuse myself, simply so you'll understand how it was. In the end, I had no choice. I did the only thing I could."

I turned my head toward the counter, where the woman I didn't know was restocking sandwiches.

"I spent years trying to make it right with Josie, and I'd very much like to make peace with her family."

Some fragment of social programming demanded that I nod here. My neck was rigid from resisting it.

"I didn't let myself think ahead to how awkward it would be."

After what seemed like a long time of me not yielding up any words, he said, "I understand that I've dropped out of the blue on you. I can't expect you to decide anything now."

Decide what? Whether we could all play happy families now Josie was conveniently dead? If I hadn't been so far away from whatever parts of myself produced speech, I might have asked. Or I might have told him, with all my fundraisorial tact, that what came next depended on him getting out his checkbook. I might have done half a dozen things, but instead I sat like a lifeguard keeping watch over an empty lake.

He reached into the inner pocket of his jacket and pulled out a small, leather-covered folder, which he opened on the arm of his chair. Like a miniature, old-fashioned desk, it held a silver pen, a pad of paper. He wrote out a phone number and tore off the sheet without leaving a shred clinging to the pad. "If you'd like to call me, or if anyone else in the family would—" He set the paper on the arm of my chair and stood. "I'd like very much to stay in touch with you, but I think it would be best if I leave the decision to you." He tucked the folder back into its pocket. It was an expensive gesture, not one you could make with a Bic and a spiral-bound notepad, even if you had an inner pocket to tuck them into.

"Thank you for making the time to talk with me. I hope you'll call."

He didn't offer to shake hands. He couldn't be sure I'd hold out my own hand, and I couldn't have predicted it either.

I watched him leave without figuring out if I should have said goodbye. At the curb, he waited for the green light to take him safely across the near-empty street, a small man with white hair and an aura of comfort.

"The rich are no happier than the rest of us," Josie told me once when I was a kid, "but they are more comfortable," and it was true that David Freund didn't look happy, just insulated. David Freund, Josie's brother, the terror of my childhood, crossing the street with the light like any other cautious old man.

I folded his phone number into the pocket of my jeans and searched myself for some feeling to match the occasion.

Finding none, I sipped lukewarm coffee, killing time until I could be sure he'd cleared his car off the street in front of Josie's house. I called Jack to ask if I could stop by after work. I felt the need for grown-ups, and from the time Josie had her first stroke, Jack and Raymond's house was where the grown-ups lived.

Raymond was pulling singed chicken out of the broiler when I got there, and Jack was sprinkling bagged salad onto three

plates and dressing it up with cucumber slices and tiny toma-
toes. Both of them cooked. Neither of them was good at it.
Raymond claimed it was deliberate. He had the makings of a
great cook but didn't want to become a gay stereotype.

I waited till we were settled before I laid out the shards of
my last two days: the hole in TOCK's budget; David Freund's
appearance at the door.

"And the thing is? The thing is, I told Claudette I'd talk to
him about money, but I had this scenario in my head where
I call him up and we have a rational conversation, and I don't
flatter the man but I don't insult him either, you know? And
then he just shows up and I won't even let him in the house,
so he has to walk with me to the coffee shop. You know the
Mound?"

"You didn't."

"It's the closest place. And I didn't think about it. But
they've got this art exhibit. Disembodied breasts."

I started to giggle and they caught it like an infection.

"And he's sitting there—"

I had to take a second run at this before I could get the
words out.

"He's sitting there in this suit."

I waved my hands to cancel that out.

"Not a suit. A sports coat."

For some reason, a sports coat was funnier than a suit.
Breasts. David Freund. A sports coat. An inside pocket. I'd
gone beyond giggling now and my mouth was locked into
the grin of hysteria. I ran my hands over my cheeks, massag-
ing the muscles toward sanity.

Raymond wiped his eyes with a napkin.

"It's not that funny," he said and started giggling again, which got me laughing so hard it hurt. To stop, I took a long, slow breath and searched for balance the way you do after a bout of hiccups, when your muscles still want to spasm.

Jack had already sobered up and was waiting for us to talk sensibly.

"Okay. Not funny. Not at all funny. I'm going to be serious now."

A flutter of laughter winged its way through my abdomen, but it was nothing more than twitching muscle. The humor was gone.

"He wants to meet us. Any of us. All of us. He doesn't give a fuck which of us because we all look alike. And I not only didn't I ask him about TOCK, I could barely make myself look at the man. He's telling me what a beautiful name I have and I'm sitting there like some sulky thirteen-year-old."

"Ick," Jack said.

"Not ick exactly. He passes the skin-crawl test. It was just sad. And then he's saying things like 'I thought it would kill me,' and 'You'll understand how it was,' and he's doing this whole dance as if we both know what happened, while I'm sitting there like a tree stump."

"Sweetheart, it's possible to ask."

"He'd tell it his way, though, wouldn't he?"

"His way's the only one left. Josie kind of abdicated there."

A sadness – David Freund's, mine, whoever's – settled over me.

"I have to call him." And that, I realized, was what I'd come there for, so I could talk until I heard myself say that. "I have to talk with him when I've picked the time."

"If you see him, do you want me to go with you?" Jack asked.

"Oh, shit ya."

"Are you going to tell Caro and Zanne?" Raymond asked.

"I expect we'll have to."

Jack looked professorial saying this – that odd balance of distance and passion he managed, as if it had all happened a hundred years ago but still had something to teach us. Which he could explain.

"Can we wait till after we've talked to him?"

"We'd better do it quickly, then."

9

I n the morning, I took David Freund's phone number out of my earring box, where I'd stashed it, and I stared at it, planning the parts of the conversation that didn't need planning, avoiding the ones that did. He'd say hello. And then I'd say hello. And then I'd say my name.

He liked my name, or he said he did.

Did I believe him?

Halfway.

A little less than halfway.

Did I care?

A little less than that.

I could have put his number into my phone but I hadn't. I couldn't stop him prowling around the house and the family – I'll huff and I'll puff and I'll blow Josie's walls down – but I didn't have to allow him into my phone. I ran through the hellos again and heard his voice in my head, gentle and perfectly poised. I'd say, "Coffee." I'd say, "Jack." I'd suggest a different coffee shop. Someplace near him. Someplace without breasts.

If I'd wanted, I could have thought up seven reasons the call could wait – or better yet, should wait – but I wouldn't have believed any of them. Besides, he weighed on me. I wanted him off my shoulders.

And if I didn't call soon, he'd dig deeper into the family. I wasn't the only descendant of Josephine Freund Dawidowitz.

When I did finally call, I didn't say "coffee" quickly enough because he said "dinner", which was the meal we called supper but with two generations of starched tablecloths and expensive manners behind it. Already he'd chosen the restaurant, and this wasn't some burger joint we were talking about, because he'd make a reservation. He was delighted Jack was coming. He remembered him as a little boy – such a happy child – and why not this evening?

Jack showed up at the house wearing jeans, running shoes, a parka, and he found me dressed as Fundraiser Barbie. I pointed at his shoes, the hems of his jeans.

"Can we do that?"

"He's the one who wants to see us."

I could have changed and done the full Fuck You Barbie in jeans and a snagged sweater, but I needed to be taken seriously and someone had made a rule that you won't get taken seriously without the right clothes. It didn't matter who made it or how bizarre it was, it was loose in the world and we all lose points if we ignored it. And anyway, Fundraiser Barbie carried a bag she'd loaded with brochures, and I needed them, even if they were no more than fairy dust and photographs on expensive paper.

"I was going to wear my floor-length gown and tiara," I said.

"So was I but Raymond got them first. Am I driving?"

He was, and I settled into the passenger seat. I could have been twelve again, or six, or fifteen. Jack was taking me to a movie, a street fair, a museum. I was in my furious teenage phase and he was getting me out of Josie's hair for a couple of hours, although he'd never have told me that was the goal.

"Did I ever tell you how much I hated museums?"

"That's why we went," he said. "You were a little barbarian and they were good for you."

I couldn't keep the patter going, though, and let silence close over us until I said, "I wish I'd told Josie I was sorry for all that time I fought with her."

"She knew."

"She told you that?"

"She didn't have to."

"Y'know, a nice, sociable lie wouldn't hurt you once in a while."

"You wouldn't have believed me."

"Probably not."

"You had reasons to be angry, kiddo. She understood that."

"Well, in case you decide to die in the next twenty minutes, I'll tell you, then: I am sorry."

"It's okay. I never got the full brunt of it anyway."

Something in me wanted to keep apologizing, as if it would rewrite me into an easier kid, because weren't we supposed to be healed when we said the things we'd been holding back? I didn't feel healed, though. If anything, I felt more ashamed than when I started.

Although somehow or other I also felt softened.

"You have a plan for this?" he asked after a while.

"We're past the point of plans here."

He half laughed, took a left turn, took a right. Headlights went past, and stoplights, and the grain silos keeping watch by the railroad tracks, in all their grim magnificence. Enough color and motion to lose myself in. Jack talked about plans – not specific ones but plans in general: what they were worth, what they weren't worth. Nothing I disagreed with but nothing I had to listen to either. In another mood, I might've thought it was profound. Tonight, it was just Jack playing the professor in his off hours.

When I was at the U., I liked to sit in on his lectures. Registering for his classes would've crossed a line, but we'd agreed that sitting at the back of a lecture hall was okay. So I knew he could snatch theories out of the air, and that a lot of them were good.

"If David Freund was anybody else," I said when he left me a longish space, "he'd be a sweet old man, but he's not anybody else, and whatever I do tonight I want to keep faith with Josie."

I listened to myself and the words *keep faith* sounded as overblown as the lyrics of "Beloved Comrade". What purity it took not just to say them but even to think them. What innocence. What stupidity.

"You will."

I turned toward the window and worked at not weeping while he drove us closer to David Freund.

At the gentrified edge of downtown, I directed Jack to the parking ramp David Freund had told me to use. I had an impulse to park someplace else and prove we could, but it was too complicated to bother. And free parking was free parking.

"He said to bring the ticket in and they'll validate it."

Jack gave his version of Josie's bitter laugh but tucked the ticket into his wallet.

"To those who need it least shall free parking be given."

"He told me what a happy child you were."

"Oh, I was. I was Caro's little brother. Every moment of my childhood was fucking ecstasy."

It was hard to think of Jack as young and hurt and desperate for Caro to love him. It was one of those things I knew in my head but could never know in my bones. Jack had always been grown and had always kept an inch of air and irony between himself and the world.

The restaurant we walked into had the dark paneling and honeyed light of old money, and if the diners weren't happy, they were more than comfortable. And better dressed than either of us. Even the ones who hadn't dressed up. We gave David Freund's name to the host and he validated our parking ticket. No waiting to make sure we bought dinner. Their clientele could be trusted on these things.

David Freund's exact invitation had been, "Let me take you to dinner," leaving no space for me to make a grand gesture at the cash register this time. Not that I could have without doing a Fukushima on my budget. He might just as easily have said, "Let me show you what Josie made you miss out on."

I was grateful to her. I couldn't get a full breath in this place.

The host led us to David Freund's table and pulled out my chair with the soul-shrinking certainty that I'd sit. We were trapped in our roles, and mine was to be as useless as an overstarched duchess while all around us and mostly out of sight the real people worked at tending us.

It wasn't that expensive restaurants were new to me. I'm a fundraiser. I know how to blend with the overprivileged. One time, I had lunch with an arts donor at a restaurant overlooking the St. Croix River, and he ordered a bottle of wine that cost well over a hundred dollars and then carped about the price. However much he donated after that, it would never have been enough.

Jack and Raymond liked nice restaurants, but they used coupons – half off if they spent twice as much as they meant to.

This wasn't a coupon kind of place.

The one percent, the Josie in my brain said, using a phrase from the Occupy movement that the real Josie had never used. She divided the world into classes, not percentages.

David Freund had gotten to his feet to greet us, and now we were seated he settled back into his chair and smiled, making no gesture we could refuse. He said Jack's name, and the sound was warm and nostalgic.

"I remember you so clearly. You were—" He indicated a height and he shook his head: the impossibility of words, the beauty of the child Jack was. "It was such a long time ago."

"You bought us candy."

"Josie used to scold me for it."

"She never minded us eating candy."

"Oh, she had her rules. *Limits* I suppose would be a fairer word. She said it was too much. Which always struck me as ironic, since when I was young she bought me as much candy I could eat. She was afraid for your working-class purity,

I think." He beamed at us, inviting us to take the side of more candy, of less Josie.

"Zanne used to get sick." Jack had gone grim-faced, as if we were talking about something life-threatening. "She'd eat hers all at once."

"Perhaps I've been unfair, then."

Jack nodded, as stiff and ungiving as I'd been at the coffee shop, and now that he was the one doing it, the absurdity of it shredded my conviction that we had to act this way. This was a human being we were dealing with – one who was full of regret for whatever the hell had happened. Would the world be one milligram better if we made him suffer for it a bit longer?

Waiters and buspeople filled our water glasses, delivered bread and menus, asked about drinks. They were young and crisp and beautiful, every one of them. They were also, every one of them, white. I'd have had to invade the kitchen before I'd find a different color scheme.

David talked us through the menu – what he'd had, what he'd liked, neutral chatter to make the time slide past.

I asked for the lone vegetarian entrée. I'm not a committed vegetarian, but it struck me as the least complicit thing I could order.

The waiter left us to our perfectly ironed napkins, our discomfort, the wine Jack and David Freund were sipping. David Freund asked about all Josie's children, as he put it.

Zanne was a singer, Jack said.

"I've followed her career. A beautiful voice. She deserves a wider audience than she's found. My mother was musical. Did Josie tell you this? She had a fine ear, a real taste for classical music."

What Josie had told me was that their mother taught piano when she was young but gave it up when she married. Married women didn't work, or not respectable ones anyway. And she never played when Josie's father was home. She didn't think she was good enough, and maybe he'd said as much. Josie never heard it, but he was the kind of man who could have.

"Caro runs a recruitment agency. Her husband's an accountant."

"And you?"

"I teach. Twentieth-century American history. At the U."

He turned to me.

"And Summer?"

"Fundraiser."

In spite of my insights, I was bristly enough to kill the one topic I wanted to pursue, leaving a stretch of awkwardness while we searched for something we could talk about. He asked whose child I was, and the question managed to offend me, although I'd have been every bit as offended if he hadn't asked.

"Zanne's. I grew up with Josie and Sol."

He sensed danger and let that slide past with a nod of acknowledgment.

A server brought salads, perfect arrangements of miniature leaves and sharp, crumbly cheese, with tiny constellations of pomegranate seeds glowing on top. In the silence while she was setting the plates down, my mind remembered arguing for TOCK's revolutionary potential when it would get us a donation, but what David needed to hear was that it was moderate. He could support it safely. And that was every milligram as true as the opposite argument, although logic insisted one of them had to be wrong.

I'd hauled out the revolutionary argument with Zac and Shar once, defending the usefulness of what I did for a living, but they wanted an all-singing, all-dancing revolution. They didn't think TOCK was wrong, but it bored them. They couldn't see a way to make the leap from tutoring kids to overthrowing capitalism.

I couldn't either, but then I couldn't see a way to make the leap without it.

If I'd asked Jack, he'd have told me revolutions happen as much by surprise as by planning, although if they're going to succeed some group has to be ready to move into an opening when it appears. TOCK wasn't the group for that, but at least it did something useful while we waited.

Besides, I wasn't sure anymore that revolution was my goal. It might be necessary – capitalism wasn't going to pack up its wares and go home just because we won a debate – but revolutions have so many built-in ways to go wrong. I'd started to think about revolution the way I thought about death: It was inevitable, but that didn't mean I looked forward to it.

David Freund tilted the smallest margin toward us.

"It means a great deal to me that you've come here tonight."

"I'm sure you understand the" – Jack searched for the word – "conflicted feelings we bring to this." The wording was so formal, it could have been David Freund's.

"All the more reason to appreciate it."

His smile was as sad as it was beautiful.

"I think this is where I admit to having an ulterior motive." I tried to smile but gave up before it went too far wrong. "I want to ask if you'll go on supporting TOCK."

A pause. He rested his fingertips on the table edge in a delicate, almost tentative gesture. We hadn't any of us touched either our salads or the bread, as if it was gauche to come to dinner hungry. I'd eaten breakfast lifetimes ago and I'd forgotten lunch. I convinced my eyes to look at something other than our food.

"I never did support TOCK, as you call it. I supported Josie."

"Who used the money to support TOCK."

"That was her choice, not mine."

It was Jack who said, "It's not a choice you were unaware of."

"That's true."

For all the story's missing pieces, certain elements of the David and Josie tale were fixed in family legend, and one of them was that in the early years Josie had sent him TOCK literature, with a note explaining that his money had created this. She wouldn't let anyone – least of all him – say he hadn't known.

As much as TOCK depended on his money, especially in those early years, she'd have been relieved if he'd stopped sending it.

"Let's not argue," I said. "This is difficult enough."

David smiled upon me like the sun smiling on ripening fields, or god on his creation. Or something else ridiculous. It was too much for the little I'd given him, but all the same I felt the kernels of wheat swell in his warmth.

"You're right. We didn't any of us come here to argue."

That left us to find something we could do instead. Jack tore a piece of bread, scattering crumbs on the tablecloth. I dug into my bag.

"I brought some brochures and such if you want them."

"Why don't you leave them with me, then? I'll think my way through this later. In the meantime we can enjoy each other's company."

I set a packet of TOCK publications on David's side of the table. That freed us to pick politely at our salads, and I made myself set the fork down between bites as if I kept forgetting I had food in front of me. I'm not a slow eater, but it seemed like the way I was supposed to behave. Zanne-like, I felt the presence of the child Josie had once been – the airless good manners that made that cold, open field so inviting, even before she'd heard the song or met the Gypsies. Or, in her case, the Reds.

Reclaiming the fork I'd abandoned on my plate, I conveyed a bit of cheese and lettuce passionlessly to my mouth. Eventually, a server picked up our empty plates. A second one scraped breadcrumbs from the table in front of Jack, deleting the evidence of his transgression. David Freund smiled at us. By coming there, by sitting across from him, we had filled his life with delight, and without consulting me, my face smiled back.

David's face didn't have Josie's strength but instead an easy warmth that was foreign to her, as if he'd always been treasured, never doubted that the world was organized for his benefit. The son and heir, the center of the universe.

In spite of that, and in spite of myself, I liked him.

*

We left while the maître d' was helping David Freund into his coat, and we didn't talk to each other until we were sealed into Jack's car and had clicked our seat belts into place. As if David Freund might still be listening.

"So what do you think that man did?" I asked.

Jack shook his head.

"Nothing he's telegraphing."

"He is gay, though, right? I didn't imagine that."

"You couldn't tell?"

"Your wavelength, sweetheart, not mine."

"I wouldn't say mine, but definitely someone's. Or he would've been back in the day."

He started the car, surrendered his validated ticket. I ran through, again, what David had said at the Mound about trying to kill himself, although I was ninety-nine percent sure I'd already told him. It seemed to need another visit.

"At least I think that's what he was telling me. He doesn't have Josie's bluntness, does he?"

"Makes you wonder how they came out of the same family."

"I expect Josie worked at that."

He took us onto the interstate, toward the home Josie had made with Sol, away from David and his validated parking tickets.

Instead of dropping me off, Jack came in. I made us the coffee we'd refused at the restaurant, and we sat in Josie's living room while it cooled in our cups, taking the occasional sip to justify having it, but it was a prop. What we wanted was to work our way back to our normal selves.

Or at least that's what I wanted, and it didn't seem like a bad fit for Jack.

"Okay, he's not ick," Jack said, going back to the first conversation we'd had about him. "Or not the way I thought. But at the same time he is. There's something—" He looked up at the ceiling for the words he needed. "He's like a thin layer of sponge covering a knife."

"I don't see the knife."

"Take a tight hold and you'll find it. It's where he's like Josie."

"Josie would never have cut your hand."

"Not yours she wouldn't've. And not mine. But in a political fight? She had an edge."

Caro came to mind. She didn't have Josie's restraint.

"Why is it we always think about the ways we're like Josie but not the ways we're like Sol?"

"Who's *we*, kiddo?"

"Okay, me. How are you like him?"

"He taught me to measure a fight instead of jumping in. To think about it, and if I still wanted to get in there, to figure out my best entry point. It's been useful. I don't think any of us inherited his gentleness."

"You did."

"Don't think so."

I could have argued but didn't feel the need.

"I like hearing it, though."

I touched my lips to the coffee without drinking. Jack had slid down in his chair and his feet stretched toward the center of the room. He wasn't a tall man – we're not a tall family – but it gave him an illusion of height.

Eventually, inevitably, we came back to David Freund. Would he donate? Wouldn't he donate? What would it mean that he was inserting himself into the family? And what the hell had he done? Was it about sex? About money? Was it the Red Scare? Would it change our decisions if we knew?

What *were* our decisions?

We didn't have any answers, so we drifted into talking about the past. Josie, he said, felt guilty about Caro.

"She asked me once if I knew what Caro needed from her as a kid, and I didn't really. Except, you know, everything. A nice, normal family. In beige. Preferably washable."

He stared at the wall for a while, then remembered I was there.

"I didn't tell her that."

"She didn't feel guilty about Zanne?"

"About the way she was with you, sure, but it was different. What Zanne did, she did as an adult. And she wasn't angry at Josie and Sol. Or she was, but it came and went, the way it does with anyone. Being angry at them wasn't her entire way of being in the world. Caro, though? Caro's always been angry. So, different category of guilt."

I nodded, one adult talking to another, not some kid eavesdropping on the grown-ups. David Freund faded into the background and the family reshaped itself into the one I'd always known.

"Josie knew I was gay long before I came out to her. Did I tell you that already?"

"You did."

"When I came out to Caro, she said, 'Figures,' as if I was only doing it because it was the theme for some lefty fashion week."

He played with his cup. A bit of silence slipped past comfortably enough.

"The whole polyamory thing, though. Josie had trouble with that."

"Everybody had trouble with that. Right now, I'm having trouble with that."

"I wondered if you were going back to them."

"I'm wondering about it myself."

He waited. I waited. I was dancing on the far edge of what I'd been willing to think and wasn't sure where my next steps would take me.

"Part of it—" I decided not to say what came next, then said it anyway. "It all looks kind of silly lately." My hands turned the cup I wasn't drinking from. "It's not that who you sleep with doesn't matter. It's not that you can't change the culture. I don't mean that. Gay liberation did. Feminism did. The civil rights movement did, although you could argue yes and no on that. But the Household? They're so damn full of themselves. It all seems—"

I ran out of words again and waited for a new shipment.

"Overblown."

I was borrowing his description of "Beloved Comrade" again, but it fit, so I repeated it. "It seems overblown. You think Josie and Sol ever sounded like that?"

"Ask David Freund and I'll bet you he'd say yes."

And with that he was back in our lives. We were living in one of those kids' puzzles, with a great-uncle hidden in the wallpaper pattern. Until you picked him out, he was invisible. Once you did, though, you couldn't not see him.

Josie Freund Dawidowitz

1953

10

JOSIE and Sol were asleep when the phone rang, and she'd gotten out of bed and held it to her head before she was fully awake.

A voice said her name.

"David?"

The voice sobbed, and that seemed like confirmation: Yes, this was David, although he'd never been a weeper, even as a child. It took her a while to orient herself, to clear the dream-fluff out of her brain.

"Are you drinking?"

He'd never been much of a drinker either, but there was something uncorked about this. Sol was awake by now, lying on his side and watching her through the bedroom doorway. She shook her head at him to say she had no idea what was going on.

"I had to do it," David said. "I didn't have a choice. You understand that."

"Had to do what?"

"First tell me you understand."

"Of course I don't understand."

"I love you. Whatever happens, will you remember that? They didn't give me a choice."

A frozen calm settled in her belly, as if her body knew who *they* were before her brain caught up.

After David hung up, she kept her grip on the phone, still trying to untangle the words she wanted. Then she settled it into its cradle and came back to bed.

"I think we've got problems."

I think. As if he'd left room for doubt. It was a reflex, giving David leeway she wouldn't give anyone else.

Sol groaned, which meant he understood. They lived in the shadow of the FBI, the House Un-American Activities Committee, subpoenas, blacklists. If the Rosenbergs – that most ordinary of left-wing couples – could be accused of stealing the secret of the atom bomb, how could anyone feel safe? Who knew if she and Sol wouldn't wake up some morning and find they'd been accused of sending Russia floor plans of the Pentagon?

She curled back into bed, facing Sol, doubling the pillow under her head.

"He was drunk," she said.

It seemed to mark how bad this was.

"Sweetheart, I am so sorry," Sol said. As if she'd told him David was dead.

That tore a sob loose and she moved closer. He wrapped an arm around her so she could mourn, but her body wouldn't go on crying. She lay silent against Sol, grateful for his solidity. He was a short, wide man – not fat but broad-shouldered, broad-chested and -hipped, with a pelt of black hair on his torso. Like a chunk of the earth itself. Everything David wasn't, and she loved them both.

"I don't know what I'd do without you," she said.

"Just as well."

They lay still for a while, neither of them kidding themselves that they'd go back to sleep. The streetlight spilled in at the edge of the curtains.

"What do you suppose happens next?" she said after a while.

"Depends what they got him to say. And who 'they' are exactly. We'll find out soon enough."

Another silence. Already they'd been to a lawyer and had papers drawn up. If anything happened to them, a friend would take the kids. Not anyone from the Party – someone less vulnerable. They wouldn't be bounced around like the Rosenberg boys.

"As long as immigration doesn't get into it," she said.

"They can't deport me to a country that doesn't exist."

Sol had been born in the Austro-Hungarian Empire and brought to the US as a baby. It was the only country he knew. English was his only language. But even so, he was a naturalized citizen, and it made him vulnerable. She found his hand and wrapped her fingers through his.

"I hope you're right about that."

"I'm right."

She hadn't asked the lawyer about it. He wasn't an expert on immigration law, and she hadn't wanted to say the words, as if the faintest breath would set the process in motion. She'd never told Sol, but there were nights when she thought her way through the mechanics of packing up the household, telling the kids they were moving to some country with a language none of them spoke, a culture they didn't understand, where they'd patch together a life that would never feel like their own in a place that would never be home.

She hadn't once imagined Sol leaving without them. They were a family. If that meant being a family of deportees, they'd be deportees.

Outside, a car honked, one long, angry blast, and when it stopped it left a silence in which it was impossible to believe anything could break through the shell of their house – the two locks on each door, the glass, the curtains and shades, the plaster and lathe that had stood since 1911.

"I should check on the kids," she said, but didn't move yet.

Sol put a hand on her hip.

"We'll get through this."

Instead of comforting her, it told her how much he thought she needed comfort.

"One way or another," she said.

She owed him that – the show of strength. She owed it to the kids, to the comrades. She patted his arm, confining the grimness she felt to the set of her lips, and she tied her robe around her with a sense that the belt was holding her together.

People had faced worse, even if she hadn't.

In Jack's room, the bed was empty, and panic flared through her before she remembered to look on the floor. He'd taken to dragging pillow and blanket there after she'd tucked him in, using the thin Mexican rug for a mattress. *Foolish*, she told herself, meaning her panic, not Jack teaching himself to make do with less than he had. She crouched beside him to pull the blanket higher, although it was fine already. She needed to do something for him while that was still possible. Of all the kids, he was the one who reminded her most of herself. She'd never slept on the floor – not that she'd have been allowed to – but she understood what drove him there. It pierced her in a way that was both warming and sad, and she knew that, if she could ease his path through the world more, she'd do it, no matter what he wanted.

In the girls' room, upstairs, Zannie – her sweet Suzanne – lay curled in her blankets like a kitten in a basket of warm laundry, trusting Josie and Sol to keep her safe, not a thread of consciousness testing the air for danger. Her breath snuffled through a stuffed-up nose. On the other side of the room, Caro heaved herself upright and announced, "I want bacon," before crashing back into her pillow. Josie pulled their blankets straight, touched their hair, allowed herself to be soothed by the normalcy of it all. The family was whole, the doors were locked, the world outside couldn't reach them until morning. Breath flowed in and out of their bodies, Zannie's clogged and rasping, Caro's so quiet she had to listen for it.

She thought Sol might be asleep too by the time she got back to the bedroom, but he asked what time it was.

"Almost four."

He groaned – for the lost sleep, for the illusion of safety the phone call had shattered.

"Caro wanted bacon."

He managed a laugh. The things Caro wanted in her sleep were a joke they allowed themselves when the kids were out of earshot.

"At least it wasn't diamond earrings."

She curled against him and would have told him about Jack on the floor, but it touched too close to something in herself that she had no words for, that some impulse protected even from Sol.

"We'll be all right," he said. "It's not the Rosenbergs, just your garden-variety hysteria."

She pulled his arm over her shoulders and sometime toward dawn, briefly, they slept.

Days passed. They worked, came home, tried not to worry the kids, slept badly. Caro lost a tooth and argued that one of the girls in her class got a dollar for hers and she should too. It was only fair.

"Her parents have more money than we do," Josie said.

"They don't."

But her voice acknowledged that the argument was lost, and that maybe they did. It was all so normal, Josie could almost convince herself that nothing had happened, that nothing would happen. Sol brought a stack of paper home for the kids to draw on. He worked for a printer who was left-wing enough that they counted his job as safe.

When the storm finally broke, Josie was trying to explain the purpose of punctuation to her class. Any year she taught third grade, one of the kids asked if they had to use it. Every year she used a variation on the same example.

"Don't you want to eat, Grandma?" she'd written on the blackboard.

She was about to erase the comma – "Don't you want to eat Grandma?" – when the door opened and the school secretary said she was wanted in the office. It was such a strange phrase that everything went into slow motion. She dropped periods into odd spots between the woman's words. She was wanted. In the office. She was. Wanted in the office. Then time compressed and she thought one of her kids was dead, Sol was dead. Then she thought nothing. She and the secretary changed places and Josie walked through the school corridors, the click of her heels echoing off the walls, marking how alone she was.

Two beef-fed men in suits filled the principal's office, diminishing the principal into irrelevance behind his own desk. Someone had brought in an empty chair and one of them extended a hand toward it, motioning for her to sit. She stayed standing as if this random fleck of self-determination made a difference. They didn't need to introduce themselves, but they did anyway: they were from the FBI, which one of them proved by flashing something she was too far away to examine and what the hell difference did it make anyway? She laughed, not to demonstrate anything but because it was all so absurd and she was as surprised by the laugh as they were. Sol and the kids were alive, and she was so dangerous that FBI agents traveled in pairs to talk to her.

The animals came in two by two, the elephant and the kangaroo.

"Mrs. Dawidowitz, we'd like to talk to you about the Communist Party," one of them said. It didn't matter which one. They were as interchangeable as two socks.

"Why? Did you want to join?"

A tiny jolt ran through the room – she wasn't supposed to say that – and the laughter drained out of her, leaving her wrong-footed and shaken. Had she just told them she knew how? Not exactly, but this wasn't the time to be creative.

"Please, why don't you sit down?"

"Thank you, I won't be staying."

That was her mother's voice, starched and ladylike, in this most unlikely of habitats. Her body had no memory now of how it had brought about a laugh. Humor was as unattainable as flight. Or motion, because it would have been a good time to turn and walk out.

"Your brother assures us that you could tell us some very interesting things."

"My brother can kiss my ass, since he's already kissed yours quite thoroughly."

From a dizzying distance, she heard the words and thought what a horrible image that was. She heard the principal gasp, "Mrs. Da*wid*owitz," as if bad language was the most shocking part of the conversation. She smiled, and it was as genuine and as unexpected as the laughter had been. The principal was a gently rumpled man, on the downhill side of fifty, waiting out the time until he could retire. His desk was heavy with papers: the place where new ideas circled the drain. Having successfully said her name, he stammered a few incoherent syllables before saying, "Under the circumstances, I don't think—"

The circumstances. Were they a visit by the FBI, or the discovery that she could swear?

He stood, and this seemed to give him access to a new handful of words. "I think it would be best if you don't return to the classroom until I've had time to consult—" He gestured to one side. He had no idea who to consult. Anyone, as long as they'd make a decision for him.

"You can expect me to do some consulting of my own."

Not that anything would come of it. The courts would be against her, as any lawyer would tell her, and so would the union, but she wasn't going down without a fight. Or if she couldn't mount a fight, at least a good, solid threat. She closed his door behind her, picked up her coat and purse, heard her heels echoing off the walls one last time, and emerged into the 10 a.m. sunshine of a clear fall day. Air flowed through her lungs, carrying a memory of last night's rain, a scent of earth, a promise of new beginnings. Relief sang through her muscles. Her body believed not that disaster had struck but that it had missed her.

She stopped at a café near the bus stop, sitting at the counter, and asked for coffee and a sweet roll. One last treat before the paychecks stopped coming. The waitress moved with a blunt grace, no motion wasted, filling the cup, lifting the roll from under its plastic dome with silvery tongs. She was as ordinary as she was beautiful. And what would she think if she knew why Josie was here on a workday?

Josie imagined herself working as a waitress somewhere. Unless the FBI made sure she lost that job too. They did that sometimes – pursued a person through job after job. You couldn't predict who they'd do it to.

She took a sip of coffee, a bite of roll. The bitter against the sweet, neither one complete without the other. The small luxuries. She should have said something about freedom of speech before she walked out, or freedom of association. She should have quoted the constitution, the Bill of Rights, Tom Paine. Not because it would have made any difference but because it would've left her thinking she'd done her part.

Hell, she might as well have quoted a comic strip for all the difference it would make.

She had a paycheck and a half coming. The words she'd left punctuated on the blackboard came back to her. She'd never have a chance to take the comma out, and that meant the kids would remember the words and wonder why she'd written them. The brightest would think their way through them and find the logic. The rest would have to learn the importance of punctuation from someone else. Or it would stay on that long list of things they did because once upon a time someone had told them to.

It felt like a betrayal not to have gone back and said she wasn't leaving them by choice. Two of the kids had just started to open up, to think she might be worth trusting, and here she was, disappearing from their lives without so much as waving her fingertips in a goodbye. Nobody would have stopped her if she'd gone back. Nobody was guarding the door and she had nothing left to lose. Her job was already dust.

What stood in her way, then? The easy habit of obedience. Lack of imagination. Years of training to be a good girl, all resurrecting themselves. David's phrase came back to her: They didn't give me a choice.

There was always a choice, and the ones that mattered weren't the ones they gave you. Would it have made a difference if she'd told him that, not when he called but long ago, when he still thought she knew everything?

He'd always wanted life to be easy.

She supposed, in a detached sort of way, that she still loved him, but losing him seemed as inevitable as losing her job.

He hadn't given her a choice.

*

That evening, she and Sol told the kids – the FBI, her job, they'd be fine, it was nothing they had to worry about.

"But if any strangers ask about me or Sol or who our friends are, you don't have to answer them. Just say, 'My mother told me not to talk to you.'"

Jack nodded, eager to step into this grown-up role. Caro agreed, but every line of her body said she couldn't do it. Josie's fear wasn't for herself and Sol, it was for Caro: if she talked to the FBI, she'd think she'd done the family some terrible damage. Jack would be fine, and Zannie was too little to worry about. It was Caro who needed a protection they couldn't give.

Should she have let them go ahead and talk?

No. The FBI would ask who their parents' friends were. She doubted they had any names the FBI didn't already know, but who could say? People could be hurt. Lives could be damaged.

Lives had already been damaged.

Two weeks later, a money order came in the mail – no note, no return address – for more than her salary had been. She had a part-time job by then, not as a waitress but in a bookstore. It was a cut in pay but they'd get by. If the feds didn't show up, she'd pick up more hours eventually. Or she'd get hired at one of the more progressive private schools. Already, she'd put out some feelers. She was able to look at the money order without longing.

After she got the kids to bed, she handed it to Sol.

"It came in the mail."

"David, David."

"So he can tell himself he hasn't done any harm."

Sol's hands turned the paper over as if he was checking for a tripwire.

"We can't let ourselves be beholden to him." He set it on the coffee table, sighed, leaned back. "Although it would solve a lot of problems."

"And create a lot of others."

He reached for her, and she kissed the top of his head where the hair was thin. It seemed like a long time since they'd reached for each other like this. The tensions. The sense of defeat. The small economies. Not to mention the kids. It was hard to say what it had been. They hadn't been fighting but they'd edged away from each other, and she leaned into him with relief.

In the morning, she sent the money order back, and three days later it reappeared with a note: "Not mine."

"Not mine either," she wrote, and sent it back again.

On Saturday morning she and Sol dozed while the kids played in the living room. She rose to the surface to hear them shushing each other and dove down into sleep again. *Just five minutes more, please.*

She surfaced again – a minute later, half an hour later, a geological age later – to rustling and more shushing. Caro's voice carried, even when she was trying to hold it back. She'd have made a great street-corner speaker.

Josie tied her robe, half her mind still burrowed under the covers, and found the kids on the floor, paper fluttering from their hands. In front of the couch, they'd made an entire town out of open books – walls, streets, a few ceilings, although they'd left most of it open to the sky. At their ages, David had owned a set of wooden blocks he could build with, every shape a child could want, all supplied for him. Pride in their inventiveness warred with a fleeting wish that she'd been able to buy them blocks.

No, it was a choice. She could have bought them blocks. The problem was that buying blocks meant not buying something else, and blocks hadn't been at the top of the list, but she hadn't been without choices.

"Look, Josie," Caro said. "It's money." She picked paper off the floor and let it flutter down again. "It's money. Really." She was as awestruck as if she'd been filtering stars through her hands or letting fairies take flight from her fingertips. She gathered bills off the floor again and let them rain down.

"Where did you get that?"

Josie heard the sharpness in her voice and saw Caro's face close itself off.

Jack pointed to their three-season porch, and when Josie didn't react he held up an envelope.

Josie forced her voice into a gentler tone: "I know who this came from. It's not meant for us." She gathered the money and straightened it but couldn't stop herself from making a rough estimate: the gas bill, the electric bill. Maybe the wooden blocks the kids hadn't thought to want but that she wanted for them. Or whatever toys were fixed in their minds as the keys to happiness. The lie she'd told them stuck in her mouth as if she'd been sucking a penny. She tucked the money back in its envelope, ran a hand over Caro's head.

"Sorry, sweetheart. It's not ours."

Caro's face stayed locked.

More discussions with Sol after the kids were in bed. The envelope lay on the coffee table as if they had to keep it in sight, and Josie was furious, a day's anger pushing against a lifetime's self-control.

"I'm going to have to call him. Or go over there. I'll go over there and give it back."

"I don't think you should see him, Josie. Really I don't."

His voice was even, as if he'd seen all this before, although who the hell had?

"There's nothing he can do beyond what he's already done."

One eyebrow went up and he didn't need to say it but he did anyway.

"Nothing within the realm of truth, no."

"You think this is something more than David trying to work out his guilt?"

"Probably not, but I still don't think it's safe to see him."

He was wrong, she thought, but in these times, what fear was too crazy to take seriously?

The money went back again, and returned to them through the mail this time, in a box wrapped with brown paper. He'd sent a note: "Will you for God's sake keep the money? You may not have noticed, but it's useful stuff. David."

It was Sol who said, "What the hell, maybe we could keep it," and it took two nights' worth of conversations for Josie to agree, but even then, they filed the note in case they had to prove no one was leaving Moscow gold on their porch. It felt silly, but nothing they could imagine was more improbable than the cut jello box Julius Rosenberg was supposed to have given his brother-in-law so he'd be able to identify himself to a Russian spy.

The next month, there was more money. And the month after that, until Josie and another blacklisted teacher used it to start TOCK. It covered two half-time salaries and a spare room in a neighborhood church. As long as they were open about where the money came from, she and Sol told each other, and neither of them finished the sentence.

Every month, money appeared, steadily outstripping inflation.

"If only he treated his workers half as well," Sol said.

Summer Dawidowitz

2012

11

DAVID Freund waited a day before he called – an amount of time I was sure he'd calculated carefully – and he introduced himself now as David, lodging himself in my head that way, paring away some shred of the separation I'd been holding onto.

Just before he called, I'd gotten an email from Caro asking when Jack and I had planned to tell her he'd been in touch. We'd been quick enough to say he wasn't family when we hadn't wanted anything from him.

And what about Zanne? she asked. We hadn't told her either, had we?

As if Zanne gave a fuck.

As if I could predict what Zanne gave a fuck about. I hadn't written back yet and wasn't sure I would. If I waited, maybe Jack would answer for both of us. Or answer for himself but draw her fire away from me.

"Could you find the time to come by this morning?" David Freund asked. "We should talk about the material you left with me."

I found the time. I was meeting with a theater company

in a week and I needed to give some thought to what they did and who their audience was, but thinking was an accommodating process. It didn't have to be done right then. And the family was due to go through Josie's things, but not until afternoon.

I showed up wearing what I'd been wearing when he called: jeans with a bit of hardened glue on the knee; a gray sweater with a dangling thread I'd been meaning to pull to the inside but never had. If we were on a first-name basis, it was time I looked like myself. Besides, it was a weekend.

His house was on Lake of the Isles, not far from where my super-radical lived, a modern one-story built to a more human scale than some of the neighbors' places, which could have passed for embassies. Come spring, the earth around it would bloom, promising every form of happiness humans reach for and never quite grasp, but now it looked as stark and unloved as Josie's.

He offered me coffee, tea, something alcoholic, his voice casting a bit of sparkle on the alcohol.

"I know so little of you. What do you drink?"

"Coffee would be good. I don't have much of a taste for alcohol."

He pushed open a swinging door and said, "Celia, could we have coffee and some of those little cakes you made?"

"Of course, Mr. Freund."

Celia. Mr. Freund. Josie nodded bitterly inside my head. She knew this world. She hadn't expected anything better from it.

David led me through a Fabergé egg of a living room to a sunroom that was marginally plainer but still terrifyingly formal. The thought danced across my mind that he kept this part of the house for display while his real life went on in the back somewhere. These weren't rooms where you slouched or put your feet up.

Celia brought us a tray with cakes no larger than tulip bulbs, each one in fluted blue paper, and china cups so thin I'd have been afraid to wash them. She was in her fifties and Latina, and she moved like a shadow through Mr. Freund's home. On each saucer she'd placed a spoon marked with a scrolling *F*. The Freund family fucking silver. I'd never stopped to think about it as real. David smiled a thank-you without breaking off what he was telling me, which was that the sunroom was a friendlier place for two people than the living room, didn't I think? He'd always loved it. It was why he'd bought the house. He asked how I liked my coffee – he hadn't noticed the other day – and told me his mother had read a book on child-rearing, god help them all, and didn't believe sweets were good for children. She doled out a single chocolate a day, each one a little larger than a nickel.

"Josie bought me all the candy I could eat when she took me out. Forgive me. I told you that, didn't I? Or ice cream in the summer. The problem was that I had to eat it all before we got home. It was terrible training. It made a glutton of me."

I pictured the small boy he must have been and the teenage Josie playing at motherhood. However little mothering she'd given him and however much more she'd given me, I was jealous of his portion. He held the plate out for me to take a little cake and I peeled away the wrapper and picked off thumbnail-size pieces, rich with dried fruit, while he told me that when he was ten and Josie was twenty he could still spend time with her openly. By the time he was in his teens, though, he had to invent stories to account for his time, because she'd become a Communist and broken with the family. He wasn't allowed to so much as speak her name at home, never mind admit that he saw her.

"Speak," he said. Not "say".

"They were awkward, those visits. I wasn't a little boy anymore, and we didn't quite know what to do together. She'd become political and wanted to – introduce me, I'd have to say. It's a more neutral word than *recruit*. She wanted to introduce me to that side of her life, but it didn't hold any interest for me."

His coffee sat untouched in front of him, and his cake was still nestled in its wrapper at the perfect center of his plate. He held the serving plate out to me a second time.

"My mother taught us never to say, 'Won't you have another?' because it might make your guest feel greedy, or think you were counting." He gave me a radiant, conspiratorial smile. "Won't you try one of these little cakes? They're delicious."

I took another cake – they *were* delicious – turning over the way he'd refused the word *recruit* but managed to drop it into the conversation anyway. He let his fingers play on the fluted wrapper of his own cake.

"I'm not supposed to eat anything interesting. The doctor spoke quite eloquently on the subject. If I restrict my diet to foods I don't like, it seems I'll live forever. Unfortunately, I'm not convinced that I want to live forever."

He peeled away part of the paper, smoothed it back into place, peeled it away again in a sort of striptease, watching intently as the means of his death came into and out of view. Then he set it down and looked at me.

"I told you, I think, that I tried to kill myself after the FBI came to see me."

The FBI, then. Who else could it have been but the FBI?

His voice turned the words into a statement but he waited until I said, "You did," making myself sound as steady and sober as someone who Josie had trusted with the story, from beginning to end, complete with all the little detours along the way.

"It's surprising how hard it is, and how much the organism wants to live. I closed the door behind them and I thought: Pills? Car? Knife? Bridge? Of course, I hate cold water, I don't like heights and I had no pills – either fortunately or unfortunately. I didn't think I had enough gas in the tank for carbon monoxide, although I had no idea how much I'd need. I still don't. Instead, I got extremely drunk and held my hand over the kitchen sink. I'm sure that tells you how far I was from being able to complete the act. I wasn't going to get blood on the carpet."

He gestured toward the living room, where a handsome oriental rug rested on the parquet floor. He was smiling again, as if he was talking about some bit of foolishness an acquaintance had gotten up to.

"Or on the kitchen tiles. I got out a steak knife and made a few passes above my wrist, and after a while I did manage to draw blood." He drew his left sleeves back an inch – the sports jacket, the crisply ironed shirt cuff.

"I didn't even leave a scar. Do you believe in an afterlife?"

I shook my head, no.

"No, I wouldn't have thought so. I wish I did, sometimes. Not the reward/punishment model, but a place where our histories drop away, along with all our mistakes, leaving – well, I don't know exactly. Whatever's left once all that's gone. Something pure and unspoiled. Isn't that what the soul's supposed to be? My parents went to synagogue and kept the holidays, but it was more a matter of convention, I think, than belief. At least, if they did believe, they never communicated it to me."

He stripped the paper off his cake and lifted it toward me in a kind of toast.

"To the afterlife."

I raised my eggshell of coffee and drank to something I didn't believe in. He didn't either, so it felt honest enough.

"If I'd had a method as pleasant as cake and coffee, I'm sure I would have taken it, but even at my age it's too slow to be of much use."

He took a small bite and set the rest down, making it even slower.

"What did you actually tell them?"

The question felt harsh, hanging there between us.

"Nothing they didn't know already. They had her name. They had Sol's. All they wanted to do was implicate me." His eyes shifted to some distant point, then they came back to me. "They used me to hurt her. To show how much power they had. Nothing more than that. Now, I've talked far too much about myself. Tell me about Summer. It's such a pleasure to know you. You're Zanne's daughter."

It was one of those non-question questions – an outline he wanted me to fill in, one that had nothing to do with what he'd told the FBI.

"Technically. Josie and Sol raised me from the time I was little."

He said, "Ah," and it could have meant he understood, or that he might have known, or only that he wasn't sure what else to say. I might have already told him this much. I couldn't remember.

"I conflicted with one of her gigs."

This earned me a small laugh. Celia came from the kitchen to ask if we'd like more coffee.

"Oh, why not."

She'd brought the pot. Either she already knew the answer or she'd have poured it down the drain if the answer had been no. Or drunk it herself. It was good coffee. Better than I'd tasted before and better than I've had since. Was Mr. Freund the kind of employer who'd begrudge her a cup of the good stuff? The Josie in my head was silent on the subject. We said our thanks, David barely looking up to address them to her, and then she was gone – a whisper of attendance, no need to interrupt our thoughts for her.

"And what about the rest of your life? Are you single, involved, married? Do you have children?"

"No children. No marriage. Beyond that it's – complicated."

Another laugh.

"I do understand complicated."

And here, as I always did when the topic came up, I hesitated, taking a quick reading of the emotional weather, both my own and the outside world's, before deciding whether

141

honesty was worth the effort it took. Today's weather demanded it.

"I have a partner. And she has a partner. And he has a partner."

That fell into a silence that wasn't long from one end to the other but felt bottomless.

"The world is indeed a strange and wondrous place."

"And we live together. Or we did until I moved in with Josie after her first stroke."

"Has that been difficult?"

I understood him to mean the relationship, not moving in with Josie.

"The hardest part is talking to people about it. Or not talking about it. Before gay liberation, being gay must've been like that."

"Not at all. You didn't talk about it. You didn't live together. For the most part, you didn't really have relationships."

I nodded to make up for my stupidity – I did know better – and the nodding made me feel sober, false, almost as brittle as the cup in my hand.

"There was someone once, briefly. A very beautiful man." He shook his head, saying no to something he seemed to be regretting all over again. "It would have made us too noticeable."

I nodded some more, maybe to say I understood, maybe just to balance out whatever his head had said no to.

"How did Josie—" he asked.

"Deal with it?"

He echoed "deal with it", trapping the words inside quotation marks.

"She and Sol had already been through the whole gay thing with Jack, so that part was easy. The multiple thing? She learned to live with it."

I nibbled my cake, sipped coffee, turned the spoon in my fingers with a sense of unreality – a Freund family teaspoon, right there in my hands – and ran out of things to fiddle with. He allowed himself another tiny measure of cake and the same amount of coffee.

"When I knew her, she thought she was sophisticated because she understood that such a thing as homosexuality existed, and because she allowed herself to say the word. And because she moved through a world where a man and a woman could have sex without the benefit or otherwise of marriage papers and be almost open about it, but behind the facade she was as closed as – well, as our parents, really. And almost as naive. The full range of human sexuality wasn't something she cared to explore, and my own wasn't something I felt free to talk to her about."

The Freund family teaspoon was back in my hands and one finger was rubbing the *F*. David let out a sigh like an engine lowering the internal pressure and said, "The FBI," letting the words stretch out into a silence.

"It's odd, but sitting here now, I feel almost dispassionate about it. At the time, though, it was the most absolutely humiliating thing that had ever happened to me. It wasn't just the stigma, how it would have affected my father, the threat to the company—"

He lost himself in something outside the window, breathed the faintest of sighs and brought his attention back to me.

"Josie told you about the company."

Another of his half questions.

I supplied the name: "Broadway Fashions."

He nodded.

"I think I might have faced all of that, but they had photographs. Can you imagine, being shown pictures of yourself? They were – graphic. Now there. Suddenly I'm not dispassionate. They were not how I wished to see myself, never mind have others see me."

He lifted his coffee and the cup wavered the slightest bit before he set it back down.

Something about his poise, his polished surface, kept me from imagining he'd ever had sex – with men, with women, with his imagination, without his clothes. Whatever it was they'd taken pictures of stayed as closed to me as it had to Josie.

"But that's in the past, and maybe it's best to leave it there. It's not something I talk about. By the time I had my little – shall we say encounter with the steak knife? By then, they'd already gotten everything they needed to destroy Josie's career and our friendship, so in the greater picture, even if I'd been more resolute I wouldn't have spared anyone except myself. Although my death might have sent a message to Josie about how I felt. She'd have been more forgiving, I think, in my absence."

A weight I hadn't known I was carrying lifted off me. He didn't want my forgiveness. He wanted Josie's.

"That's probably true."

"So there it is. You came in with no illusions, so I trust I haven't disillusioned you."

"You haven't."

For a moment, behind his softness I caught a glimpse of the steeliness he shared with Josie – an ability to look at his own failings and not turn away. It wasn't the knife edge Jack had warned me about, just the raw material you'd need to make one.

"But you wanted to talk about TOCK. I've read the materials you left me, and it's not a bad organization – it's not training suicide bombers, it's not blocking roads and bridges – although I doubt it will make the least bit of difference in the world. For – what's it been? – fifty years, sixty years, they've been organizing parents to improve the schools and I wouldn't say we have a world-class system yet, would you?"

"It does what it can."

"Of course it does."

I rummaged through the ragbag of my mind for some less weary scrap of argument and found nothing, but it wasn't as if what I said here mattered anyway. This wasn't a conversation, it was a one-person performance with well-measured gaps for audience participation.

"I'm deeply conflicted about donating directly. It's not the same as giving the money to Josie."

"It amounts to the same thing."

"Not to me."

"I don't know what I can say to that."

"You still think you can change the world, then?"

And that's when I quoted Margaret Meade at him: "Never doubt that a small group of thoughtful, committed citizens can change the world. Indeed, it is the only thing that ever has."

He sighed as if he'd heard Josie say the same thing, year after year, inside his head. As if I'd confirmed his gloomiest beliefs about me: I was just one more lint-brained lefty.

"And what about Summer?" he asked. "Does she have any needs of her own?"

"She manages," I said. "But she's here to talk about TOCK."

Some small bit of my mind played with the sounds of *TOCK* and *talk*, then went on to *tick*, and if David Freund had started tick-tocking it wouldn't have struck me as any more surreal than the two of us discussing my needs in the third person.

But why limit ourselves to Summer's needs? Did she have any wants?

Yeah, she had a few. She wanted to put her feet on the couch and strew crumbs about like the Queen of the May strewing flowers. If the Queen of the May did strew flowers. What did Summer know about the Queen of the May?

David nodded his disappointment. He should've known I had no needs of my own. I was Josie's granddaughter, and pure in soul.

If I could've afforded to, I'd have told him to go fuck himself.

Okay, I wouldn't have, but I felt better thinking I could.

"Perhaps if I visited the organization and got some sense of what it does," he said.

With a feeling that Lake of the Isles' waters were closing over my head, I said of course, that was a perfect idea. The lake was frozen solid enough to drive on, but never mind, I felt them close over me anyway. I'd just agreed to spend more time with him. We talked about when he could drop in at TOCK's office without disrupting either tutoring sessions or meetings. His tone was as soft as before, but if I wanted to do business, these were his terms.

At the door, he turned charming again. Or not *turned.* He hadn't been not-charming. But the change was there all the same. He told me how much it meant to have seen me. He invited me to stop by again. He told me – and it wasn't a request – that we'd stay in touch, that he looked forward to meeting the rest of the family. My eyes wandered to a painting on the wall behind him, a dark landscape in a frame so elaborate and golden it turned the painting into an afterthought. It was pretentious and sad, and if anything could turn those breasts at the coffee shop into a valid artistic choice, this was it.

I made myself look at him and did my best to like him. It was both easy and impossible.

"Let me take some time to think about the issue you've raised."

I was nodding before I understood that the issue was TOCK. Was money.

Had I done anything but nod and eat little cakes since I'd been in his house?

"I'll be in touch," he said.

I nodded some more. All the moves were his.

To the south of David's house, on the next lake in the chain, the park board had a concession stand where Josie and I used to buy ice cream when we went to the beach. Calling it a *concession stand* had felt very grown-up and it had left me with a special feeling about the place. It was closed for the season, but I parked as close as I could, pulled the zipper on my jacket that last inch toward my chin and walked to the lake's frozen shore. Looking for Josie's presence, Zanne would have said, but it was more like measuring her absence. You can trust absence. It won't let you down.

The sun was strong enough to make me squint but carried no hint of warmth yet. I tried to imagine myself forward to the time when the ice rotted and the city closed the skating rink it had cleared, but it was too far out of reach. I lived in January. It would always be January.

Did Summer want anything?

Now David wasn't around, I rediscovered my ability to want, and hell yes, I wanted to own Josie's house – all of it, not just my quarter. And miracle of miracles, not far from where I stood lived a relative with a stifling amount of money, while here, toasty warm inside my jacket, was a want that money could grant. Not a need, but not some passing whim either. I wasn't lusting after truffles or a chance to see the earth from space. If I introduced the aforesaid want to the abovesaid relative, would he grant my wish?

He made it sound like he would, but didn't the wishes in fairy tales always find a way to go wrong? Nobody ever read the fine print.

I packed a snowball and threw it onto the ice, half expecting to throw my greed away with it, and when it didn't leave I sat on the frigid bench, wishing my jacket was long enough to tuck under my thighs.

Jack had said I'd keep faith with Josie, and he'd made it sound so simple. Of course I'd walk right side up. What else could I do? But if I was going to keep the money flowing into TOCK's bank account, I'd have to dance attendance on David, and he'd dangle toys in front of me as if I was a kitten, and sooner or later one of them would get to me and I'd snag my claws in it. It wouldn't matter if it was something for myself or if I held out for what the organization needed. Hadn't I been fake enough to find some genuine liking for the man when I needed it? How much phonier can a person get than to cover the false with the real?

Back when I imagined myself beside Che in the mountains, good and bad had been identifiable and separate. Maybe that was what marked us as adults: not the size of our bodies and the number of winters stacking up behind us, but the ways good and bad flowed into each other and the difficulty we had in separating them. The interpenetration of god damn opposites, although I doubt that's what Marx had in mind when he came up with the phrase.

If it *was* originally his. I could ask Jack if I ever needed to know.

My mind went back to Che, to the fact that he wasn't even alive when I built my stories around him. And back when he had been alive? He'd misread his time, his place, his whole damn strategy. The peasants didn't come flocking to him. He and his – yes – comrades spent more time keeping themselves alive than making a revolution. If I could've run to them, what would I have been joining? A survival exercise with political mood music?

"Talking to these peasants is like talking to statues," he wrote in his diary. "Worse still, many of them are turning into informants."

An adventurer, Josie would have called him.

Did he shoot the peasants he thought were informants, or get someone else to? He couldn't have afforded not to. How much justification, then, does a killing need?

Still, the village schoolteacher who met him after he was captured, not long before the army shot him, described his gaze as tranquil, ironic, piercing and unbearable. The secular saint of my childhood. I was so sure he'd create something pure.

Sitting on a frigid bench in a park Josie used to bring me to, it came to me that Che had been far more of an imaginary father to me than my official imaginary father. How had I not let myself know that?

I thought about throwing another snowball but didn't bother getting up. The last one hadn't helped.

Did Che ever want a house? Did the revolution provide that for him and his family? If it did, was that corruption or was it realism?

By the time I left the lake, the cold had settled so deep into my bones that the car's heater couldn't touch it.

12

I WAS closing Josie's garage door when Irene detached
herself from her back porch and crossed the alley toward
me, cigarette in hand. She smoked outside. Keeping the walls
clean. Keeping the air clean for when her kids and grandkids
visited, for when one of their families moved in, as they
did when their lives fell apart, moving out again when they
patched them back together or the arguments started running nose to tail.

After Josie fell that first time, Irene started dropping in
to say she was heading to the supermarket and did we need
anything? She and Josie had never been close – they traded
a friendly word or two in the alley and that was about it –
but when I couldn't leave Josie alone anymore, it was Irene
I called if I wanted to walk to the store and pick up a carton
of milk we didn't need yet. It kept me sane, being able to go
out like that for an unscheduled breath of air.

Most weekends, Irene found a reason to knock on the
back door, and I'd make coffee. She wasn't a natural talker
and what she did say came out of the corner of her mouth,
as if she wasn't easy enough with the process to use the full

spread of her lips. Conversations were hard work and full of gaps, and half the time Josie fell asleep in her chair, leaving the two of us to manage on our own. She did that with all of us by then, but with Irene it embarrassed her. The relationship was fragile. And Irene bored her. I don't know if it was a form of snobbery, but Josie felt it was, and she'd have changed it if she could have. The last thing she wanted was for Irene to know how she felt.

Irene was tall and rangy, but she made a habit of taking the rocker, which was a short person's chair that left her with a lot of leg sticking into the center of the room. It was also the least comfortable chair we had to offer, but I never found a way to steer her toward the couch. I could've managed it well enough with someone else, but I wasn't easy with her either.

I locked the garage door and told Irene how much her help had meant.

"And your visits. To both of us."

She gave me a nod that meant she'd heard me, and asked about the funeral.

"The family doesn't do funerals. It's just—" I gave up on the idea of explaining it. "We'll have a memorial, but we haven't figured out when. Can I let you know?"

That was another thing that made conversation awkward. We didn't do anything the way she expected. Or the way I thought she expected, although it wasn't like I knew how to ask. We were a family with two queers, one singer, a professor, a professional who did Irene had never asked what but who carried herself like she was better than the rest of us. Not to mention a tall, dreadlocked Black man and a short dreadlocked white woman with holes in her clothes. We had walls full of books, heads full of politics that had gone out of fashion before even Caro was born, and a genetic allergy to sports. Plus we were Jewish. And atheists.

It all gave us an air of not-like-normal-people-ness.

Now, saying we'd have a memorial instead of a funeral, I felt like I might as well tell her we didn't bury our dead, we just left them in the back bedroom so we could visit when we got lonely. Still, she said okay as if she'd expected it. And maybe she had. Maybe normal families held memorials too. I knew as much about normal families as she knew about Jewish atheists.

As I thought she knew about Jewish atheists.

I reran my thank-yous, hoping somehow to bring myself, if not the rest of the family, back into the circle of normality, but she just drew smoke into her lungs and turned her head to exhale it away from us both.

"Family going to sell the house now?"

"If we can."

"Lousy time for it."

We bounced that back and forth a bit – it was, yes, completely lousy.

"You should buy it," she said.

"Love to, but I'll never get a mortgage. I work for myself. And my income pretty much tanked this last year."

"Buy it contract for deed."

I said, "Huh," and let my mind turn the idea this way and then the other, admiring how it caught the light. Then I said I'd be moving back in with the people I used to live with anyway.

"Nothing like having your own place," she said. "Besides, it's a lousy time to sell. You'd be doing the family a favor."

And as if we couldn't already have recited it, we ran each other through the list of empty houses up for sale on the block: Tony and Carole's place had been repossessed after he got cancer, and so had Bill and the other Carol's after he lost his job and they split up. Plus the house on the corner where they used to keep that dog tied in the yard, although neither of us knew what the story was there. They were just gone one day, dog and all, leaving nothing behind but the rope. And that didn't count the ones that were for sale but still lived in.

"Looks like I might be joining the club," she said.

I looked at her house as if I had to make sure that was the one she meant.

"Well, shit."

"You can say that again for me."

"What happened?"

"I got downsized back there a while." She laughed, a gust of bitter air from that one side of her mouth. "What a word, huh? God damn downsized. I'm working again – whatever happens, I work – but I got behind on the payments and you know how they tell you to call them before you get into trouble? Well, I called, damn their souls if they have any, and I asked for a what-do-they-call-it, a loan modification, and they tell me I have to miss a payment or two before we can talk about modifying, and then when I've done that they tell me I'm behind on my payments and they already sold my house, so they're tossing me out." She nodded across the alley. "Twenty-three years in my place. You believe that?

Twenty-three years of a thirty-year mortgage. I raised my kids there. How many times over you think I've paid for it by now?"

"Three times? Four?"

She shrugged, then pinched the ember off her cigarette and dropped the stub in her pocket.

"Hell if I know. More than that, probably. Whatever it is, it's not enough."

I closed my eyes and felt how deeply I didn't want to get involved in this. Whoever the world's normal people were, they said things like "Well, damn" and "That's awful" when someone was losing their house. They didn't say, "Hang on, I know this scruffy left-wing organizer with no social skills who might be able to help you."

I wasn't normal people, though. I knew Rob, and Rob worked for Occupy Homes. If Irene didn't want any part of him, that had to be her choice, not mine.

"I know someone you should talk to," I said.

"I'd talk to the devil himself if he'd keep me in my house."

"He's not that bad."

I didn't have Rob's number but I scrolled through my phone and left a message for Shar, asking her to have him call me.

He called before Irene got her gate open, and I yelled after her. Could she be home around six? Rob didn't know what weekends were. He'd stop by.

13

B y the time I got inside, I had maybe half an hour before
the family was due and I grabbed a cold potato from the
refrigerator and stared out the window while I ate – the snow
pitted and flecked with black, the toothpaste-green stucco
of the house next door. They were enough to keep my brain
away from thought.

Then the family descended: Caro first, then Zanne. Jack
and Raymond last.

I still hadn't answered Caro's email about David Freund,
but she didn't mention it. Caro had a reset button. No matter
which family member she blew up at or which one blew up
at her, by the next time she saw them she'd started over and
for at least as long as it took to greet each other we came with
no history. We'd get along fine. Until we didn't and either the
same old stuff came up or she found some new grievance.

Or – *admit it, Summer* – until I did.

We worked our way through the first layers of Josie's
stuff – the portable, the wantable, the usable, the unquestionably junkable: her unfinished medicines; a broken string
of beads, the pair of glasses she'd run over years before and

stuffed in the back of a drawer, even though the optometrist told her they were past fixing. She hadn't been able to throw them out, and now that it was up to us I didn't want to either, although I didn't make a case for keeping them when Jack tossed them in the trash bag.

Caro passed by the couch and laid a hand on the arm, where the worn spot was covered by something that might have been meant as a prayer rug.

"God, this couch. What do we do with this couch?"

"Deal with it later," Jack said. "Let's do the easy stuff today."

"Look at it, though."

"Later."

"What, I can't talk about it?"

"You can do anything you want, but what's the point?"

"I'll take it," I said.

"It's a wreck. Take something worth having."

"I love that couch."

Caro nodded as if she knew better.

"I *do.*"

"Fine. I won't argue."

It sounded like an argument.

Now it was mine, it was bigger than it had been when Josie owned it, and heavier. I'd have to organize everyone I knew to move it, not to mention rent a U-Haul. I'd have to figure out where I was taking it. But at least it wasn't going to the dump.

Zanne wandered down from the attic carrying a newborn's knitted sweater and matching cap, a pair of baby shoes so old they buttoned, and a tarnished silver baby cup. She rubbed the cup and, instead of a genie rising out of it, faint curling script appeared and she read it out: "Caroline Miriam Dawidowitz."

Caro reached for it, turned it in her hands.

"That would've been from Sylvia."

Sylvia: Josie's mother, who would have ordered it in secret, hiding the cost from her husband, and brought it over in secret, and held her first grandchild in secret. By the time Jack was born, she was dead of cancer. There were no more silver cups.

"Josie must've been furious," Jack said.

"And touched enough to keep it," I said.

"In the attic."

I echoed him. "In the attic."

"I'd like to keep this," Caro said.

Even if it hadn't been hers, she was the only one who'd want it.

Zanne handed me the sweater and cap.

"Here. You get these."

They were tiny and yellowed and handmade, and too ancient to have been Caro's. Someone in the history of this family had sat knitting for a baby who hadn't been born yet. For Josie, surely, because anything made for Sol at that age would have been handed on until there was nothing left. And it would've been in the old country anyway.

I couldn't associate such a homey act with Josie's family.

Zanne handed Jack the shoes.

"You get these."

He looked like he'd caught a football and couldn't figure out how, never mind where it came from or what to do with it.

"Some of the household things, the decorative stuff?" Caro said. "We should leave them where they are for now. They'll make the house look lived in when buyers come through."

"It is being lived in."

I might as well not have said it for all the reaction I got.

"Could we cover the couch? Summer, did she have a bed-spread, something like that?"

"I like the couch."

"We've been through that. You're not buying the house."

I excavated a Mexican rug that had been at the back of the linen closet since I had no idea when. At some point it had been my bedspread, and then it wasn't, although I couldn't remember why. It didn't cover the arms but it showed we'd made an effort. Josie would have liked the splash of color it added, even if it was a bad match for the prayer rug.

"I'll see if I have something bigger at home," Caro said.

"What does that leave?"

I listed the first things I could think of: Josie's jewelry and clothes; the boxes upstairs, which could have held anything from broken dishes to Lenin's collected works; a bunch of flowerpots and garden hoses and planters, whole and broken, in the basement. Some yard stuff in the garage.

Caro and I ended up in Josie's bedroom and we spread her jewelry on the dresser. She had a few good things I didn't know the history of and a silver necklace Sol had given her early in their marriage. After his death, wearing it took on a ceremonial quality.

"You should take that," Caro said, sliding the necklace in my direction.

"I wouldn't know what to do with it."

"You might still have a child to pass it on to."

"I will not have a child."

"Well for Pete's sake take something other than the couch and that ridiculous baby sweater. To remember her by."

I had her wedding ring.

"I don't need anything to remember her."

She made a dismissive sound – a kind of *ach* that struck me as particularly Yiddish, and in the context of our family oddly so – and she turned my palm upward, poured the necklace in and closed my hand around it, leaving her hands in place for some fraction of a second longer than she had to. It was like some secular blessing. It was like love. In spite of everything, we were family. In spite of everything, that mattered.

I hit a reset button of my own.

Then she squeezed a goodbye and got back to work, leaving my skin bare. In the cup of my palm, the necklace still held Caro's warmth and the backs of my hands called to her that they were lonely.

"I'll ask if the others will take anything," she said. "I could see Zanne wearing some of it."

Late in the afternoon, we gathered around the bagels Caro had brought – two dozen for the five of us; let it never be said Caro was cheap – while Zanne made coffee. I was too tired to stop her, and it didn't feel like as much of an intrusion with the whole family in the house. The bags for the secondhand store slumped by the front door, in the same spot where Zanne and I had set our boxes and bags and suitcases the day she brought me here and fled. We pulled bagels toward ourselves, passed each other the cream cheese, then stood like visitors who wouldn't be staying long enough to sit. Any minute we might turn away, wander into another room, walk out the door without calling goodbye. Once we cleared out the last bits of furniture, it would be up to me if I saw Zanne and Caro again. A bitter kind of freedom glimmered just ahead.

Would I miss them? The way I missed long hair once I cut it short. I felt more like myself, and it was good not to have it in my face, but it took a long time to stop feeling a coolness at the back of my neck and an absence when my fingers wanted something to fidget with. We would have liked to like each other better. They were as much a part of me as my out-of-season name.

Maybe we'd like each other better if we kept our distance, whatever that distance turned out to be.

Josie would have accepted that breaking up her house was necessary, but the breakup of her family would have torn a hole through her. She never pressed me to see Zanne or to tell her I loved her, but she did tell me once, after a second drink, that she'd hoped Zanne would find a way to redeem herself with me.

I didn't ask what it might take for her to do that, and later, when the question formed in my head, couldn't find a way to call the topic back.

Now that it was too late, the way was obvious: all I'd have had to ask was, "Josie, do you remember when you said that about hoping Zanne could redeem herself with me? What do you suppose she could have done?"

Some part of me still thought she knew a way.

And now, instead of reconciling, I was sorting not just through Josie's stuff but through her family. I'd keep Jack and Raymond. Whether I wanted him or not, I'd have David. And I'd have Shar, Zac and Tee, who weren't her family but who'd wandered onto my list anyway. If we could stay in that moment when Caro pressed the necklace into my hands, I'd want her in my life, but that never happened with her. It didn't seem like much to show for the years I'd lived.

It was a heartless way to think about human beings, and I pushed the list into some unlit corner of my mind.

Zanne delivered the coffee.

"I should tell you, I met the dread David Freund," Caro said. "He's a charming man who's had a great deal of grief in his life, and he'd like to be part of this family."

"Grief he inflicted on himself," Jack said.

They were both directing this at Zanne – they'd turned her into their jury – but now Caro turned to Jack.

"You don't know that."

"I know enough."

I knew more, and I could've told them I had a category now for what he'd done, but our edges were too jagged and the topic was too fragile. In spite of which I waited to see if I'd tell them anyway. It was like waiting to see if a glass at the edge of a coffee table would fall.

It didn't, and I wasn't about to push it.

"I told him I didn't think it would work, but if you'd give up half an ounce of your precious purity you might learn something about this family."

Already we'd learned that someone on Josie's side of the

family knew how to knit. How many surprises could we handle?

"And that would be what exactly?" Zanne asked.

"That he's not a monster. That he's an old man with regrets who'd like to have his family around him."

I thought they might go on playing tug-of-war with that, but they let the rope go slack. We were still standing, and both that and the silence turned awkward.

"Well, I tried. I thought this is what would happen, but I did try."

"Everybody," Raymond said. "Sit." He pulled out a chair for nobody in particular and Jack took it. "You too. Summer? Zanne?"

He didn't direct Caro by name, as if she'd set herself beyond his reach, but he stood until she sat, then took his own seat, pulling his coffee close as if to remind us of an ancient tradition: drink, eat, get along together, we live on a very small island and have no one else to depend on.

"I'm not exactly family, so maybe it's up to me to say this. You love each other. That gets lost sometimes, but it's why you fight."

Zanne laughed.

"That's the most depressing comment on human nature I've ever heard: You love each other, that's why you fight."

"We probably do," Caro said, "but I'm not sure how it changes things."

He shook his head over the lot of us.

"Okay, fine. I've done my guru shtick. You don't like it, go find your own guru. Just don't shed blood in the dining room. Summer still lives here."

Caro turned her head toward the windows, moving Raymond to peripheral vision.

Josie told me once that of the three kids it was Caro who suffered most when she was blacklisted, although she never knew why. Maybe it was her age, maybe it was her character.

"I never felt I could reach her after that," she said. "Not entirely. Neither could Sol. So I never knew what it meant to her."

It came to me now that knowing wouldn't have helped. Caro got a good look at the path Josie and Sol had chosen and thought, *There's an easier way and I'm taking it*. And it would have been easier if she hadn't still wanted Josie and Sol's approval.

"Should we set a date for the memorial while we're all here?" Raymond asked.

We argued dates, places, speakers, whether to leave time for anyone who wanted to talk or stick to a list, and something about the task made us gentle again. The arguments were kind ones, but even so we left the plans half-finished and instead made lists of the more manageable jobs. I promised to sort Josie's papers and let everyone know what we had. Raymond offered to scan some of the photos and distribute the rest so everyone got a handful of the originals. Jack would go through Josie's books. Zanne would do whatever she wanted and there was no point in asking her to do anything different because it wouldn't happen anyway. Caro had already talked to people she knew and narrowed all the world's real-estate agents down to one glowing example of the species, so she'd handle that, and could I stay in the house while it was on the market?

By the end, we were still playing nice. Caro divided the bagels into plastic bags, insisting that we wanted them, that we could freeze what we wouldn't eat right away, that Zanne liked the cream cheese with salmon, that I should choose between chive and plain, that whichever one I didn't want Jack and Raymond did. No one was going home empty-handed.

"Can you stay a minute?" I asked Jack and Raymond as Caro and Zanne worked their way into their coats. Raymond raised an eyebrow and I looked away as if it would keep Caro from scenting conspiracy.

When we had the house to ourselves, I told them about the feds, the photos, the steak knife.

"I'm relieved," Jack said. "I was afraid he had a taste for pretty young boys."

"Do we know he doesn't?" Raymond asked.

"He mentioned a man. All he said was that he was beautiful, but I did get the impression he was a grown-up."

A sadness settled over us. For David Freund, maybe. For how shopworn the missing part of our family story turned out to be. Of course it was politics. In our lives, what wasn't politics?

14

A T Irene's that evening, Rob rested against the arm of
the couch like a pile of laundry waiting for the iron.

I'd never been in her house before. Until Josie's stroke,
I doubt she'd been inside ours. We were a friendly enough
neighborhood – when snowstorms shut the city down, we
shoveled each other's walks and driveways; we traded gossip
in the alley; we knew who it was safe to leave a key with and
who broke all that glass on the sidewalk last year – but only
the kids were in and out of each other's houses. The adults
built some distance into their friendships.

Irene's place had hardwood floors – she'd told us about
them when her kids were pulling up the carpet and sanding
them – and every surface was swept clean of clutter. I'm not
sure why, but I'd imagined her letting papers pile up, or
plates and cups and beer bottles. Whatever objects her small
moments were made up of.

She made us coffee and Rob cradled his and talked.
Instead of explaining Occupy Homes, or talking about how
the banks had been bailed out after the crash while home-
owners were left to sink, he started in the middle, talking

about a homeowner he was working with whose place had been put up for sale illegally, while he was still trying to negotiate a loan adjustment with the bank, then about another who'd found forged documents in her file. I couldn't read Irene's reactions – she was just a woman holding a coffee mug. She could have been thinking anything. It wasn't until he talked about having been arrested trying to block a repossession that she broke in to say she didn't like that kind of thing.

"That's fine. Everybody organizes their own defense, and they do what they're comfortable with. We'll follow your lead."

"I'm not that kind of person."

He nodded as if he knew what kind of person that was and said it wasn't for him to impose anything, and why didn't she tell us what stage things had gotten to?

She blew air sideways, the same way she blew cigarette smoke, and she pushed herself out of her chair, but instead of going anywhere she looked around as if she was surprised to be standing with us in her own living room.

"I don't know what'll happen to me if I lose this place."

Rob made a sound of agreement, and three beats too late I said, "You'll get through this." Not because I knew that but because it seemed like somebody should say it, even if it was the person with the least information.

She said, "Right," not believing me any more than I did. She opened a drawer in the dining room and brought Rob a file. "I've read all of that, but I don't understand half of it."

"You weren't meant to. They pay lawyers a lot of money to make sure of that." He flipped pages, slowing down over some, flitting past others with a glance. "First thing you do, you ask the bank for your loan file. Your complete file, and look for anything unusual. That's how the woman with the forged papers found them. Or maybe that's the second thing. Any chance you can afford a lawyer?"

"You kidding me?"

"That's okay. It helps, but you can do it without one."

He went back to the beginning of the file and started over.

"I should leave you and get back," I said.

I tipped my head toward the house, although I wasn't headed there. I'd promised to spend the night with Shar. I'd only come over to introduce Rob. I carried my cup to the sink and Irene walked me to the back door.

"If you don't need me for a minute, I could do with a smoke."

Rob murmured, "Fine," his attention on the papers.

We stood on the back steps while she lit up and we stared into the half-dark alley. She tapped ashes into her palm and emptied the palm onto the snow, and we kept silent company until she'd stubbed out the cigarette and dropped the stub in her pocket. It felt companionable and oddly useful to stand in the cold with her, pulling dry air into our lungs. As if we were holding the world in place.

"I should go," I said without moving.

She nodded back toward the house.

"Are you sure about him?"

"He's done this a lot."

"It's just – all that getting arrested stuff."

"He's okay. He's just – dedicated."

"Plus he looks like he just crawled out of bed."

I thought about Che and the peasants – wrong message, wrong strategy, wrong moment. Wrong clothing. I shrugged my arrest-free shoulders to say I understood. Which I did, actually. Why trying to block a repossession would make her uneasy, but also why Rob had to do it: not because it would keep anyone in their house but because it was the only thing left to do. Because it was a line he had to cross. Because in some possible future it might make a difference to some other homeowner.

I could also see its pointlessness. I could imagine Rob finding some loophole for Irene to crawl through so she could keep her house and I could imagine her losing it in spite of a dozen illegalities in her papers. I could imagine every possible outcome, but I still couldn't imagine the end of capitalism. No thread I could find led from Irene getting cheated out of her house to Irene wanting a revolution.

Or a peaceful transition, if that was still on the menu.

She rested a palm lovingly against the door frame.

"God damn money pit," she said. "I should be glad to get rid of it."

"You're here," Tee announced before the door had closed behind me. "I'll light the candles."

The table was set with her grandmother's tablecloth and with good beeswax candles from the co-op, turning it into a household date, a time for us all to fall back in love with each other and with who we were trying to be.

Smile, some inner voice commanded. *Love.* But nothing inside me lifted. I was earthbound, clay-souled. I'd come to spend the night with Shar. No one had asked if I wanted a date night.

I hung my jacket on an empty peg, unwound my scarf, pushed my shoes off with my toes, one hand on the banister for balance. From the kitchen, Zac called a greeting. Tee hugged me, one of her you-me-this-moment hugs, the dead match still in her fingers, and walked me into the kitchen so I could trade hugs there.

"I brought bagels," I said. "For the morning."

Shar lifted a lid and stirred, releasing the scent of curry. She built her curries spice by spice, layer by layer. Zac lifted a lid to show me the rice he'd made. He couldn't cook without calling for applause, and I noticed this the way an anthropologist might, for what it said about men and women and the effort it took to change a culture. People never quite clear the shadows off their hard drives.

I carried bowls to the table. Three willow-pattern soup bowls Shar had found at Savers. A lone glass soup bowl I didn't recognize. The dragon-patterned serving bowl I bought at a garage sale when I lived alone and had no use for it. They dished out and ran back to the kitchen for one last bit of this or that until, two by one by one, we were seated. Shar got up one last time to turn off the overhead and the candles brightened.

"It's good to have you back," Zac said, and although a part of me heard him playing master of ceremonies, the rest of me heard a person drawing me into the circle of light.

"It's good to be back."

And as if the words carried the feeling in with them, it was good, and I was back. We traded news, blended into each other. They told me Rob had been arrested at another repossession, and he'd been charged with everything from trespass to riot, although the lawyer said they'd bargain it all down to something manageable. I told them about Irene's place. Piece by piece, what I loved about these people and this house reassembled itself in candlelight, in food, in voices, in Shar's hand reaching across the table to touch mine. They were good and generous people who loved me for reasons I didn't want to question, and they had love enough left over for Rob, even though he was just passing through.

15

IN the morning I slept late and came downstairs to find the members of Shar and Zac's discussion group draped across the living room furniture and scattered on the floor. I made myself coffee and sat at the kitchen table, flipping through a day-old newspaper someone had left, half listening to the talk on the other side of the doorway. I thought of the discussion group as Shar and Zac's, although Tee was part of it, along with some half a dozen other people, but Shar and Zac had started it and it was Shar who kept it going, sorting out dates, emailing reminders, ordering books when they decided to read something together.

I'd stayed out. Their politics weren't mine, and after a bit of push and pull they accepted that.

All this time after the breakup of the Occupy camp, they were still talking their way through what it had brought: direct democracy, horizontal structure, the beauty of a movement that didn't make demands. For them, the world had changed. For me, some promising light had blinked on and then off again, leaving us to figure out what we'd seen in that moment of brightness – or what we thought we'd seen.

Rob hadn't joined them. I figured he'd lost patience with their strand of the movement, or with their endless talk, which might be the same thing. Occupy Homes was about demands. The Occupy purists and the Occupy Homes people were still on speaking terms, but their differences were as visible as the crack that runs up the side of a cup long before it starts to leak. Or they were to me.

If I'd told them that, someone would've said I was trapped in an old model, the one where as soon as there's disagreement, the group splits and each grouplet accuses the other one of betrayal. And maybe I was, but even so, the cup had a crack. Sooner or later, liquid would find a way through.

In the living room, someone quoted Bakunin: "Anyone who makes plans for after the revolution is a reactionary."

The rest of them laughed.

I hadn't been listening closely enough to know how the quote fitted into the conversation, but I had an impulse to appear in the doorway like the ghost of revolutions past and announce that anyone who doesn't make plans will watch power fit itself to the hands of people who did. Some new version of Stalin, say.

And if they took me seriously enough to argue? I not only didn't have a plan for after the revolution, I didn't have a plan for the next seven minutes.

My mind slid sideways, landing in the time after the czar's government collapsed, the provisional government that followed it fell apart, and the Communists – people, I had to assume, who weren't so different from Josie and Sol, with all their gifts and their failings – held power in their hands and might still have found some humane way to use it. It was a moment when all things were still possible, or might've been.

The people who didn't have a plan didn't hold power for long. It sat like a fresh-baked potato in their unprotected hands – what the hell were they going to do with this thing? – and stayed there just long enough to leave burn marks. Then someone else had hold of it. Someone less troubled by the ways right and wrong leaked into each other, and the ways that power corrupts. Someone whose mind was a political oven mitt.

Not many of them lived long after that. The ones who survived the revolution's enemies were killed by the revolution itself.

And the decent people – not the Stalins, not the Pol Pots – who did make plans? Did any of their plans fit the moment they found themselves in? The revolution was under attack by so many armies that they color-coded them: Black, White, Green, not to mention a full range of colorless armies invading from other countries. Their own Red Army was starving, and so were the towns, the cities, anyone who couldn't grow their own food. Who has a plan for that? Famine stalked people through the streets by day and gnawed at their bellies by night.

And at the lowest level, revolutionaries – the Sols, the Josies, the people who didn't doubt the revolution but were beginning to think it should be nudged a bit to the left or the right – argued with each other, or with themselves:

– *The peasants are only hoarding food because we're keeping the prices low. Let them set their own price and they'll sell.*

– *They'll sell to the rich and the poor will still starve. It'll be like it was before the revolution. Our only choice is to confiscate as much as we can.*

– *They'll hide it and then no one will eat. Next year they won't even plant.*

– *If we don't confiscate food, we'll never see next year.*

Both sides were right. Both sides were also wrong.

– *Forget the peasants a minute. We've identified a spy. Do we shoot him?*

– *What choice do we have? If he gets the chance, he'll shoot us.*

Shooting people wouldn't come easy to the Josies, the Sols – even the Zacs. And if we agree it's necessary, where do we draw the line? Do we shoot the saboteur? The White Army soldier? The anarchist?

– *Not the anarchists. They're on our side.*

– *That was last week. Now they're against us. Besides, this one let the spy go. He remembered the time the czar's police almost shot him.*

Do they arrest the anarchist? Do they shoot him? Do they share a bottle of vodka with him and weep for what they've all become? Do they worry the question so long that someone else shoots him?

Once you start shooting people, the rifle makes its own decisions. And if you refuse to shoot, all those armies move in and shoot you. What choices do you really have? "You think you're driving the machine," Lenin said, "but it's driving you. Someone else's hands are on the wheel."

Not one of his better-known quotes.

You make plans for after the revolution, but the revolution turns out to be a different beast than the one you expected. You stocked up on hay and it eats meat. It's hungry. It's eyeing you.

– *Why haven't we turned the factories over to the unions? Why haven't we turned the unions over to the workers?*

– *Are you crazy? The workers are so hungry they'd bring the czar back for half a loaf of bread. We'll hold power in their name, in their interest. Just during this crisis. All we have to do is get through this week, this year, this century. As soon as we get breathing room, we'll figure out what socialism looks like. What we have now? It's provisional. It's all provisional.*

Until it isn't.

In the living room, the group laughed again. All the happy little protorevolutionaries. They were genuinely nice people, most of them, but what kind of society would they build? Not the one they meant to. Nobody gets that lucky, so what were any of us supposed to do? Leave the world to the managers of empire and keep ourselves pure? If the Great Recession, with its near-collapse of the world economy, is anything to judge by, the establishment doesn't know what they're doing any more than we do. And they have an accounting to make as surely as the revolutionaries do – for massacres, for famines and torture and ecocide.

A picture of Josie came to me – Josie as she was before the first stroke: tiny, certain, grim by then but still magnificent – sitting in the next room with Shar and Zac's anarchists. They'd have loved her. They'd have hated her. It would've been mutual.

Or not quite mutual. She'd have thought they were silly. Whatever they thought of her, it wouldn't have been that.

After the collapse of the Soviet Union, she accepted that the one-party state hadn't been the best choice the Bolsheviks could have made, but I never asked how she thought anyone moved from that revolutionary moment when a party seizes power to the time when it risks power passing into hostile hands in a free election – risks letting the gains it won in blood be undone by careerists.

As it turned out, they were undone by careerists anyway, only they had to join the Party and make their careers there, mouthing revolutionary pieties.

In the other room, Zac was making the same argument he'd made to me: that we couldn't let the ultraright have a monopoly on guns.

"If it's not the government coming for us, it'll be the racists, the neo-Nazis. Change isn't going to happen because we have better sex. We've got to be able to defend ourselves. Besides, some of the people I talk to at the shooting range? You'd be surprised how much common ground we have. They're worried about the little guy. They talk about who really holds the power. We need to be talking to them or only the far right will."

Voices lapped over each other.

"What they're really afraid of is Black people," someone said, rising above the noise. "They're worried about the international Jewish conspiracy. That's who they think has power."

"You've never actually talked to them."

More overlap, like static on the radio. Zac cut through to say some of them had their heads up their asses, but some of them were open to what he had to say. They worried about the same things we did.

They will eat you for lunch, I thought, meaning Zac, meaning the guys at the rifle range.

I poured another cup of coffee and stirred milk in to soften it.

The guys at the rifle range would either push Zac out or draw him down roads that weren't on his map yet. He wouldn't go for Jewish bankers, but he might believe black helicopters.

It made all of Josie's Marxism look useful. It might have been left in the sun until the plastic cracked, but it still gave her something to measure herself against. She didn't talk about the little guy and the elite, who you could define any way that suited you, but about the working class and the capitalists.

And guns? She wouldn't have ruled them out, but I doubt she'd ever shot one. They weren't the tool she needed, and as I listened to the voices get louder in the other room I didn't see us needing them either. At least no time soon. Because for all Zac and Shar's talk about revolution – and they talked about it a hundred times more than Josie and Sol ever had – they weren't expecting one any sooner than I was. Overthrow capitalism? Right after we all put down roots and flowers sprouted from our fingers. None of us had trouble imagining the end of the world: nuclear winter, global warming, pandemic, overpopulation, asteroid strike. We'd grown up with the end of the world. But the end of capitalism? Fat chance. The capitalists we would always have with us.

It was why they wanted their better world now.

I heard myself think the word *they*.

178

Your reason for wanting a divorce?

Political differences, Your Honor. I can't take these people seriously anymore.

I'd miss Shar – the feel of her breasts and belly pressing against me was as clear as the prospect of separation could make it – but I'd already left.

16

W HEN I got home, I emailed Caro. It would've been easier to start with Jack, but it was Caro I had to convince. And Zanne, but she was never the place to start.

"It's a lousy time to sell a house," I typed, "and I have a proposition for you. I'd like to buy it on a contract for deed. Are you interested?"

There. Summer had a want and she didn't need David Freund's help.

Was it "a contract for deed" or just "contract for deed"?

I stared at the screen, deleted what I'd written, hit Control Z to put it back, deleted it again, and tried to come up with something more gracious.

Grace eluded me. This wasn't fundraising. I wanted something for myself and that made it hard to call up the right tone. If Caro was interested, fine. If she wasn't, it might make my life easier.

I Control-Z'd the original back into place and hit Send. Which made me realize it wouldn't make my life easier if she said no. I wanted this house. I wanted to wrap it around myself like one of Josie's old sweaters.

A couple of hours later, I got an email back. She and Steve needed the money for her business, so no, that would be awkward, but what price was I proposing? What interest rate? Over what period? With what sort of down payment?

It wasn't a flat-out no.

I typed, "My down payment was a year of my life taking care of Josie while my own business tanked, that was my down payment," and I left the words on the screen, unsent, while I walked to the kitchen to make coffee, but all I had to do was inhale the scent of ground beans to understand coffee wasn't what I wanted. That drove me back to the keyboard, where I wiped out what I'd written.

"If you're willing to consider it, we can figure out the answers."

Send.

"And fuck you too," I said to the screen.

I'd find some other place if I had to. I'd done it before.

Of course, Josie'd been alive then, keeping this refuge open for me as surely as she'd kept David Freund outside the family.

I looked at the screen and said, "Fuck you" again.

It helped, in the smallest possible way, and reminded me I could throw my argument in her face later if I had to.

Then I wrote Jack, which I should've done first. For all I knew, he and Raymond also had plans for the money. The world we live in demands a steady flow of the stuff. How many of us could look at a chunk of money and agree to have it trickle in over decades instead, even for people we loved?

I made the coffee I still didn't want and wandered through the house with it, unable to find the traction I'd need to do something useful. I could research grants that might fit TOCK. I could work on the crowdfunding campaign for the community clinic. I could count up my hours and send out invoices. I could open Facebook and see what had happened to the friends I'd lost touch with after Josie's first stroke.

Okay, it wasn't after her stroke. It was after I moved in with Shar and Co. They drifted away. Or I drifted away and barely noticed which of us was moving. The Household and the people it drew into its orbit had been enough.

I didn't do any of those things. I told myself it didn't matter what I did as long as I stopped drifting, so I opened drawers and closets, spreading out the papers I'd promised to sort, filling a good part of the floor. I found check stubs dating back to 1964. I found water bills and the save-this-portion-for-your-records section of electricity and phone bills, which she'd dutifully saved for her records. I found income taxes, property taxes, the complete repair record of the car she sold when she stopped driving, and I sorted them all into separate stacks until I forgot which stack was which and what the categories were and had to start over. I called Jack, got Raymond, and listed some part of what I had.

"How much of this do we need to keep?"

"Shred the check stubs. Maybe the recent ones, I don't know, keep them till we know we don't need them. Shred the car. Keep the taxes, anything to do with the house. God knows why. I'm superstitious. You can always shred it later but you can't unshred it. What else have you got?"

"That's as far as I've gotten."

"Okay, call back if you want to."

I shredded, let the shredder cool down, shredded some more, wondered if there was any actual reason to shred them instead of setting them out with the recycling, and shredded them anyway, put the papers Raymond said to save back in their boxes and folders and stacked them in the corner of the living room before I hauled out another batch and found a thin folder was marked DAVID: LETTERS, with Josie's careful punctuation, even on a file folder. It held two half-size pieces of heavy notepaper. The first said, "Will you for God's sake keep the money? You may not have noticed, but it's useful stuff. David."

So he was spiky even with her, and he used expensive paper for a quick note.

The second opened with, "You say, 'You will not stuff money through my door.' To which I can only say, 'You will not tell me what I may and may not do.'"

"May and may not". Even if he hadn't signed that one, and even if Josie hadn't labeled it, I'd have recognized David's voice.

He went on, threatening to keep on stuffing money through the door until she agreed to cash his checks.

We had to be the only family on earth where stuffing money through a door was a threat.

I set the folder on the couch, marking it out as something separate, something that mattered, although what I'd do with it I had no idea. Show it to Jack and Raymond. Save it because people save things like this, hoping someone will come along and find a use for them.

By the time I dragged out the notes and newspaper clippings Josie'd gathered for her last, unwritten article, my back hurt and my fingers smelled of dust and vanished history. If the stack had been more bills and receipts, I'd have shoved them back in the drawer and quit for the day, but I remembered these. When I moved in after her stroke, she had them spread on the dining room table, which she'd turned into a desk now that she lived alone, and I left them there, waiting for her to either come back to them or put them away. After a few weeks, she asked me to bring her some. Everything was dated and stapled; each stack was labeled. She was able to tell me which stack she wanted, and it made me think her mind had found its old patterns. My computer was upstairs then, and I left her with a lapful of papers and went back to work. When I came down she'd dozed off and the top layer had slid onto the floor. I picked the pieces up, put them back in what I hoped was the right order, and when I added them to the stack on her lap, she woke up.

"I don't remember the point I was trying to make," she said. "I remember the pieces, but I don't remember what my point was."

"It'll come back, don't you think?"

She didn't seem to hear me.

"You might as well take them."

I set them back on the table, as close to where they'd been as I could manage, as if this would maintain a structure she'd recognize, but that version of Josie didn't exist anymore. The papers gathered dust until weeks later, when Caro, Steve, Jack and Raymond were coming over for dinner and she told me to put them away so we could eat at the table.

"Are you sure?"

She gave me the fatalistic nod that by then she seemed to have always had, although she hadn't.

I gathered them up in an order that might let her reassemble the pieces if the rest of her was magicked back from wherever it had gone, although I was pretty sure minds didn't work that way, or at least that hers wouldn't. Some tiny clot had blocked the flow of blood, and the argument she'd assembled and all the data to back it up had scattered like the points of light that make up fireworks. Without her mind to hold it together, it wasn't information, it was junk.

"What was it about?"

She gave me something close to a laugh.

"I don't remember."

"Nothing?"

"Special ed. Assessment, maybe. But my point? It's gone. It's just gone."

I stacked the papers, shoved them onto the bookshelves on top of a stretch of short books, and cleaned dust off the table. We ate that night in the hollow her thoughts had left.

Paging through the papers now, my hands smelling of dust, the old Josie materialized in my mind – the person who had clipped and marked and filed these. The person we'd lost.

I reached the end without figuring out what to do with them, and I checked my email to see if Jack had gotten back to me about the house.

He hadn't.

The next day, the papers still nagged at me and I called Claudette to ask if anyone would be able to make use of them.

"That was Josie's niche. I can't see anyone else doing it."

I'd known that. Josie published articles in education jour-nals, hoping they'd plant a seed somewhere, and maybe they did, but no one else in TOCK was inclined to bother. No one else's mind worked that way. They were problem solvers, she told me once, not system changers.

"It's just – I'm sitting here with this pile of papers she put together and I have no idea what she was going to do with them but I don't want to throw them out."

"Then keep them. How much space can they take up?"

It was that simple. It was that pointless. I laughed. She laughed. We hung up. Josie had left me a quarter of this house; one kind, regretful, manipulative brother; a failed revolution; and this stack of paper.

Not to mention her couch, her wedding ring and neck-lace, and her spiky family.

Had anyone ever been richer than me?

I made a few calls, shaking the trees to see if any work fell out of the branches.

Jack was due to come over and sort books that evening, and Caro emailed to say she'd be over as well. As if the two of us might pull off a coup if she wasn't around to supervise.

Be fair, I told myself. *She might want to help.*

I wasn't in a mood to be fair, and I thought about pull-ing a disappearing act. I could go buy groceries. I could buy tampons at Target and then cruise the aisles and dream about filling my cart with stuff I didn't need and couldn't afford but could so easily develop a longing for. I could take a trashy book to the Mound and admire the art. Maybe one of the walls had plaid flannel breasts, or vaginas made from dish towels. How could I call my sexual education complete if I didn't see them? As long as I had money to part with, no end of places would welcome me.

Instead, I rang Irene's back doorbell and waited in the cold, wishing I'd grabbed my jacket. The wind was blowing straight out of Canada and it cut through every gap in my sweater. I might as well have been wrapped in wax paper for all the warmth it kept in.

The kitchen light flicked on and she called through the door to ask who it was.

"It's Summer."

She turned locks – not the normal two, but three – and let me in.

"I have the most ridiculous name," I said.

"I like it."

"You never had to stand outside in January and yell, 'It's Summer.'"

"I see what you're saying there."

We were still in the kitchen. In the next room, the TV was playing some sort of soap. The actors sounded like they hadn't seen their lines half till half an hour before the cameras started rolling.

"You want a beer?"

"Nothing, thanks. Caro's coming over and I thought I'd ask about that contract for deed thing. Do you have to have a down payment with that?"

"Not that I know of. Depends who you buy from, what you work out with them. I bought this place on a mortgage."

She blew a bit of laughter out the side of her mouth. "It's supposed to be safer. My brother bought contract for deed, though, and he didn't have two dimes to rub together. Couldn't have gotten a mortgage any more than he could've gotten a job as a brain surgeon. You want me to ask him?"

"If you see him, yeah."

She leaned against the counter. I leaned against the stove, and propped up with her like that, it felt like we were a couple of kids with nothing better to do than wait while time slipped past. It was the most comfortable I'd been with her.

"You're thinking about it, then."

"I'm thinking."

"They're being difficult?"

"They're being family."

Another short gust of laughter.

"That's unfair," I said. "Caro has plans for the money. I don't know about the others."

"You ask her how fast she's going to get her money when the place doesn't sell."

I nodded as if I'd march across the alley and say exactly that. A few bits of silence stalked between us on stiff legs.

"Here," she said. "Sit. Why are we standing?"

We pulled out the kitchen chairs and sat. The TV advertised toilet paper. It was so soft you'd think you were wiping your hind end on angel's wings.

"She's a hard one, that Caro. I don't mean to talk about your family, but I'm telling you, Caro's out for Caro. She'd as soon have her hand in your pocket as in her own."

"I don't have enough in my pocket for her to bother with."

"People like that, they always find something."

I wasn't sure she was being fair, but I laughed anyway.

Back when the family argued over who was going to put in how much to support Josie, it was Caro who balked at a sliding scale. She and Steve had expenses. She had a business. We didn't understand what that was like. We couldn't just march in and expropriate.

From each according to her character.

Zanne wrote her last year's income on a scrap of paper, then a wild and irresponsible guess at her expenses, then how much she could afford every month, and she shoved it into the middle of the table. She made a speech about the kind of parents Josie and Sol had been and the kind of children we needed to be in return. Without noticing, or at least without acknowledging it, she included me as one of their children, not as hers.

Jack bargained Zanne down. Keep the amount realistic, he said. Otherwise we'll come up short.

There were months when he and Raymond covered her payment. He was the treasurer, so I was never sure how many months, but I do know about a few.

Caro, though – once she agreed, she paid what she owed. And what she wasn't told she didn't ask about.

"I never thought of her that way," I said.

"I shouldn't talk about your family," Irene said again. "It's just, you did right by your gramma. I don't want to see them take advantage of you."

I turned away, stared at the photos on the refrigerator. Her own grandkids, safely tucked under their parents' wings.

When I could trust my voice, I said, "I should go home. Her and Jack are coming over."

She and Jack, Josie's voice said. It was one of the things we'd never found a way to agree on.

"You go. Be sure she doesn't take anything she shouldn't."

"We're doing okay with stuff. It's just the money where we're running into trouble."

"Just money, hey? Nothing anyone cares about, then."

By the time I got home, they were both in the living room. Jack said he'd been wondering where I'd gone. Caro said hello and wondered nothing.

"I ran over to talk with Irene."

I could've left it there and played nice for however long the book-sorting took, but that possibility didn't present itself to me. Hadn't Irene sent me out the door with instructions?

"We were talking about contract for deed."

"I talked with Raymond last night," Jack said. "We could live with it."

"Steve and I can't."

"The place isn't going to sell in any kind of a hurry. Not till the market changes. Have you seen the for sale signs up and down the block?"

"You'll forgive me if I wait to hear that from a real estate agent?"

I sketched a shallow bow in her direction. It kept me from having to say anything.

"Tonight's about books," Jack said, aiming the words at me as if somewhere along the line we'd set out an agenda and I wasn't following it. As if he wasn't the adult I counted on anymore but some unaffiliated individual who, in the push and pull of the family, was likely to take anyone's side. "A lot of them, I could make use of. Either of you feel a strong pull toward any of the books?"

Caro and I had been trying to stare each other down and we broke off to turn to him.

"They're yours as far as I'm concerned," she said.

I shrugged.

"I get lonesome for one, you can lend it to me."

I left them to the books and went into the kitchen for a glass of juice I only wanted because it was in another room, then sipped it to prove I'd had a reason to pour it.

When I moved back in with Josie, I didn't drink juice. I hadn't since I was a kid, but Josie believed in the stuff. It had vitamins. People who drank it were well fed and healthy. Even after she stopped wanting coffee, she wanted her juice in the morning, and she wanted me to have some with her.

She was still trying to take care of me.

I swallowed what was left. It was tart and sugary and electrically orange, and it tasted of all the love and safety that had slipped out of my reach without bringing any of it back.

I washed my glass, which made me think to wash the sink. Then I washed the counter, the refrigerator door, the stove. It made a kind of sense of my life: I was the person who cleaned these surfaces, and who did it with the kind of drive I only had when I was pissed off.

Caro's voice came through the open doorway, saying that now she thought about it, the bulk of the books should stay where they were while the place was on the market. What we should do this evening was weed out the overflow, maybe give them a quick dusting.

Jack browsed, talked agreeably about which ones he wanted. This one about the Red Scare, that one on Sacco and Vanzetti. He'd check with Zanne, although he couldn't see her wanting any.

"Take the red stuff too. The Marx, the Lenin."

"A specter is haunting the living room?"

"You're not half as funny as you think you are."

Another day he would've been funny – I wasn't far enough gone to miss that – but today he just sounded brittle.

"Put it all in a pile. If no one else wants it, I'll take it." He raised his voice to call into the kitchen. "That okay with you, Summ? Pile of books in the corner?"

"Fine. Anywhere."

I opened the cabinet under the sink and hopscotched cans and plastic bottles around until I found the spray cleaner Josie'd had me buy. She understood eco-arguments in theory but never took them in deeply enough to change her habits. Germs were bad. Killing germs was good. I could probably have talked her out of it but hadn't. Kill those germs. I sprayed the stuff on my dishrag, hoping to use less than if I sprayed it on the stove itself.

In the other room, Jack's voice had a bring-us-all-together tone. Sol built such beautiful bookshelves, he said. If he could've made a living working with wood, he'd have loved it.

I closed myself into the bathroom. By the time I came back, Caro was talking about the time Josie carbonized the macaroni because someone from TOCK called and she couldn't get off the phone.

Jack raised his voice to include me.

"The house smelled for days. She sent us to the chow mein joint to get takeout."

I refused to make the sort of sound that would say I'd heard.

"Remember the ring bologna she used to buy?" Caro said.

"God, yes."

"We called it rubber-hose sausage," Caro called to me. She had a bring-us-all-together voice too, and this was it. "Awful stuff, but it was cheap. Sol had this story about getting arrested somewhere. Pittsburgh, I think. Something to do with a strike. Anyway, the police beat him with a rubber hose. Terrible story to tell kids."

"If it's what happened, it's worth telling," I said.

My voice was stiff, but it seemed important to let her know I wasn't a party to the peace treaty she and Jack had made. She dismissed me with a puff of air from between her lips.

"It was Chicago," Jack said. "Or Detroit. When he was a Party organizer."

This was addressed to me.

"A rubber hose didn't leave marks. The Red Squads used them. 'Hi, you're under arrest.' Whack, whack, whack. 'Sure you're not in the mood to leave town?'"

"You see what I mean?" Caro said. "Terrible story for kids to hear about their father. So we called it rubber-hose sausage. Because it was terrible."

"We didn't hear how awful we were being. Or I didn't." Jack's voice shifted to address Caro. "You were in your let's-see-if-we-can't-make-them-mad phase by then."

"That's unfair. The thing was, Josie loved being short of money, and it drove me crazy. We lived with all these little – cheapnesses. All because she had something to prove. And it wasn't necessary. She knew we hated ring baloney but instead of buying something else she kept finding new ways to hide it. Pea soup. Hot dish. We're lucky she didn't slice it into our jello."

"If she did," I said, meaning love being short of money, talking at more or less the same time Caro was listing the ways she hid it, "it was only to remind herself of what she'd gotten away from."

That wasn't what I'd been hoping I'd say. I didn't believe she loved being short of money, but they'd known her earlier than I had, and longer. The best I could do was pick away at the edges of the argument. And be unpleasant. When all else fails, a person can always be unpleasant.

"I'm sure that's true," Caro said. "And if it had only been for herself I wouldn't have cared, but it wasn't. She made choices for us as well."

"That's what parents do. At least when she made decisions, they were responsible ones."

Not even Caro knew what to say to that. People don't when I talk about Zanne.

"Money *was* tight," Jack said after a small silence.

It wasn't enough to get him back in my good graces, and the comment stretched out into a silence. I ran the dishrag over the oven and broiler doors, then the handles for the burners, then the broiler door again. The marks I was rubbing away might have been a few days old and might have been there for months. How long had I managed not to see them?

"Josie and Sol were an awful lot to live up to, I'll give you that," Jack said, conceding an argument nobody had made.

"I mean, what are you supposed to do when your parents are congenitally right?"

They laughed, the two of them sharing a single drive to escape the overbearing safety of their parents. Without asking my brain if it was a good idea, my arm threw the dish-cloth through the doorway.

I hadn't been aiming for them and I didn't hit them – it landed on the rug – but once I'd missed it felt like a failure.

I said, "Fuck you, Jack. Just fuck you."

"Hey," Jack said. It was a gentle sound, and he left the bookshelves to stand in the kitchen doorway. "Hey? You okay?"

"I'm fuckin' fine. Go ask how Caro is."

"I'm asking you. You know I loved them."

"Then don't make fun of them."

"I didn't mean to. Especially to you."

"It doesn't matter if it's to me or the god damn refrigerator. Just don't make fun of them."

He knelt beside me in front of the broiler and waited for me to soften, and we were ridiculous there, on our knees, worshiping the great god of the gas oven.

"She loved you," he said.

I shook my head to keep the words out, but when he put an arm around me and rested his forehead on mine, I didn't head butt him. I didn't pull away.

"*They* loved you."

Sobs wrenched themselves out of me – the hard, painful kind I used to cry as a kid.

After what seemed like a century, I stopped bawling and he brought the box of kleenex from the bathroom. When he passed me one, his hand smelled of dust, of pages that hadn't been turned in years.

"The sausage wasn't *that* bad."

I managed something like a laugh.

"It's just – we decided we didn't like it and after that we had to not like it. You know what kids are. She probably didn't serve it as often as we think she did."

By the time we moved onto the kitchen chairs, something nameless had changed and I was as clear as the sky after a storm. In the next room, Caro moved books, piling the most screamingly left-wing ones on the floor, busy not hearing us, busy believing the sausage was as bad as she'd said it was and that Josie cooked it once a week through every year of her childhood, but Jack had separated from her. She might as well have been in the next county. He sat across from me and talked about having wanted both more and less when he was a kid – more toys, more stuff, nicer clothes, but also the toughness of the kids who had less – and the problem was that he couldn't have them both. It was complicated. The kids who had less wanted more, so if he wanted it too, wasn't he being like them? Except that if he got it, he was even less like them.

He talked about how Josie and Sol occupied the revolution so completely that nothing he could do mattered half as much.

"In the sixties—" He stopped, started over. "I wasn't much use as an activist. Even before I started studying history, temperamentally I was already a historian. I liked that distance. Organizers have to be tough. When I teach the civil rights movement, the anti-war movement, gay liberation, the women's movement, everything else that happened back then, a few of the students get starry-eyed. And I want to say, 'Hey, it's not like that. It's all meetings till two a.m. and arguments and accusations and someone getting arrested and someone else doing something stupid just when you think you've got it all sorted out, and not knowing if it'll work anyway, and wondering which of the people you trust is actually a cop. It's feeling like the whole world disagrees with you. It's scary as hell. And you lose. Over and over again, you lose. Things do change, but never enough and it always feels like you're losing. The power's on the other side. You need to know that from the start or you'll never last.'"

I seemed to be listening not to my uncle but to the person Jack was to himself. He'd been young. He'd measured himself against Josie and Sol, decided he could never match them, and stepped back.

"We'll figure it out about the house, okay? There's no rush, is there? Because you're right – it's not going to sell in a hurry."

No, no rush. Only that it was driving me crazy. Other than that, though? None at all.

"It's not about the house," I said, and he didn't ask what it was about. Which was good because I had no idea what I'd have said.

Sol had told me about the rubber hose once. I'd have said it happened in Detroit, but I couldn't swear to that and it didn't matter anyway. He told it to me as a bedtime story, before he had to stop climbing the stairs and started saying his goodnights at the door that kept heat from escaping up the stairway. My mind never formed the thought that a bed-time story should be any different. I was tucked up and warm and Sol was stretched out on the empty bed across from me, talking into the dark about that unimaginable time before I was born.

Wasn't he scared? I asked.

"You can't imagine how scared. It's not that I'd never been in a fight before, but they'd been kids' fights, the kind where you walk away with a split lip, something like that. Some of the guys I was with, though, they'd been through it before. They were tough. But me? My mother didn't believe I'd live through a winter unless she put the mittens on my hands herself. You know what I thought when two guys grabbed hold of me and the third one came at me with that rubber hose? *They want to hurt me!* As if in the whole world, I'd never thought anyone would want to do that."

The hardest thing he ever did, he said, was not leave town once they let him out of the police station.

"And you want to know the truth? If it had just been me standing on the sidewalk, I'd have been gone. But they weren't so bright. They let us all out at once and I was too ashamed to look those guys in the eye and say I was going home."

By the time Caro and Jack left, the bookshelves were showing a few bare patches and I rearranged Josie's tchotchkes to fill them: a lumpy bowl Caro had made; one of the spun glass horses Zanne collected when she was still trying to fit in with the other kids; a smooth rock from Josie and Sol's first trip together. All the parings of family life – things that should have felt like company but screamed of loss instead.

When I was a kid, I couldn't imagine owning anything as significant as that rock. I couldn't imagine making anything as skillful as that lumpy bowl.

Shar called and asked if she could come over and I said yes, then hung up and gave myself instructions: *You have to tell her. You can't not tell her.* But what I wanted wasn't to break up with her but to magic back the time when knowing she was on her way set every cell in my body dancing. When it pushed back the claustrophobia of walking Josie from table to armchair, from armchair to bathroom, from bathroom to bed, from bed to table.

Didn't we have the right to one more night together? Once I'd told her, there'd be no going back.

But from the time she came in the door we were like ragged fingernails, scratching where we'd only meant to touch.

Was I moving home or wasn't I? she asked.

"I can't."

The words were dictated by some process so far out-side rational thought that I had no idea where it had set up camp. If I could've unsaid them, I would have. I tried to call up the sense of family that had been so important when we first moved in together, when we promised to blend freedom and commitment, love and politics, home and world, theory and practice, coffee and cream, bacon and eggs, except that in deference to Tee and Shar we weren't going to have meat in the house. But sitting in Josie's newly fragile living room, Zac and Tee didn't feel like family. Not even Shar did. They'd fallen away from me like dried mud. Family wasn't something people could just declare because they'd charged up their hormones and their politics. Family was genetic fucking fate, that's what it was. It was loss. It was time – more of it than the four of us had accumulated together. Decades, maybe. I didn't know how long, but longer than we'd had.

And all the same, I reached a hand out and touched Shar's arm.

She moved away.

"I thought you were headed that way."

For no reason that made sense to me, I didn't want her to have known that and was half tempted to say I'd move back so I could prove she'd been wrong.

We sat staring at the walls for a while.

"I should go."

Her voice was smaller than usual, and less certain. This wasn't the Shar I was used to. She was supposed to be—

Okay, she was supposed to be more like Zanne. In her drive. In – I turned my head to one side as if it would block the thought that was forming – in the way she saw what she wanted and didn't stop to think it might not work for me. She'd always been clear that she needed more than just me, that Zac and Tee weren't negotiable and neither were a few extracurriculars.

I'd told myself it would work.

She hadn't gotten up to go yet.

"I thought the way we're living meant something to you."

"I thought it did."

My voice was even smaller than hers, a tiny sound in a huge silence, as if something in my throat was blocking the passage of – not quite a lie, but not quite the truth either. I didn't tell her the whole project had started to look silly. I stored the thought inside me, where it registered in a voice very much like Josie's.

How much had Josie herself left unspoken? Was that kindness or dishonesty?

"I love you," Shar said.

She reached across for me, and every part of me reached back – hand, arm, lips, tongue. I hadn't noticed that my stomach was a clenched fist but now it opened, and I opened, and when we broke off the kiss I pressed her hand to my cheek and said I loved her too.

And I did love her. Nothing about that was less than true.

We went to my bedroom, moving as carefully as barefoot kids who'd just shattered a glass. Is it safe to put a foot here? Is it okay to put a hand there? Then our bodies remembered each other and we fit together as well as we ever had, the slow dance of touching places that weren't supposed to be sexy and were all the sexier for not having been overused. Her shoulder blades, the palm of her hand, the folded skin soft inside my elbow, until we couldn't hold off any longer. I reached for her hip, traced the fold between buttock and leg, reached inward. She shifted toward me – keep going, reach further – and my brain kicked in, telling me how good we were together, that we could keep seeing each other even though I'd broken up with the Household. I could be an extracurricular.

Or we'd break up but go out on a high note. It wouldn't matter what happened after this one long moment together.

We'd hold that note inside ourselves and it would sound there forever. Except I'd already let the note go flat. I didn't belong in bed with her anymore, and I couldn't touch her as if I did. Not because I'd never lied in bed – there'd been a few times when an odd kind of pride had kept me going when I should've stopped – but I was too raw for it this time.

I pulled away from her.

"I can't do this."

She crashed onto her back.

"Oh, for fuck's sake."

"Well I'm not going to lie to you."

"God, no, don't lie."

She pulled her clothes on, arms punching through tangled sleeves, toes catching in the rip at her knee, and I memorized her – the small mound of her belly, the breasts so flat you didn't notice if she was wearing a bra or not, the white-girl dreads I'd never said anything to her about. I'd miss her. I knew that, and even so a weight lifted off me.

That night, I let the TV play until I fell asleep on the couch, and when I woke up I tried to slide into bed without breaking the spell, but somewhere between the couch and the bed sleep had broken away from me and I lay with my eyes closed, missing first Shar and then any generic partner. I was alone in my bed in a house that wasn't mine. I was alone in a world that was coming apart. Weeping seemed like a good idea, but I couldn't even do that.

17

B Y the time Caro's real estate agent – that one agent who'd be able to sell Josie's weary house in this even wearier market – came to see what she had on her hands, I hadn't gotten used to Shar's absence, but I had gotten used to the uncertainty about how long I'd be able to live there. Wasn't uncertainty our natural state of being? Nothing was permanent. Look at Irene's house, bought on a mortgage because that was safer. Look at the Household. Weren't they going to be family for the rest of my life?

For the unforeseeable future, I had a place to live. What more could I want in this wavering world of ours?

I could want David Freund to call with a donation.

What the hell, I could want wings. Nothing stopped me from wanting wings.

Caro showed up before the real estate agent, and before she'd even bothered to take her coat off she'd straightened the Mexican rug on the couch and moved the armchair an inch to the left. Then she hung up her coat and brushed away the toaster crumbs that either I'd missed or she'd imagined.

"I'll give you a hand if you want. What needs to be done?"

"It's fine. You go ahead and work."

I couldn't work, though, not with her twitching this thing and brushing that one, but I went back to the computer while she pretended she could turn Josie's worn, comfortable nest into a desirable property.

When she reached the dining room, she nodded at the mounds of paper that collected, more or less of their own accord, around my computer.

"Could we put that in a drawer for the time being?"

I hit Save as if it would preserve some sort of order in my life.

"We'd rather not. There's a system here. Can't she point her camera in the other direction? She won't want the computer in a dining room picture anyway."

"I'll ask."

She didn't move on, though.

"What?"

"When she shows the house—"

She stopped there, looking for a way to finish the sentence. I could've said, "*If* she shows the house," but it didn't seem worth the effort.

"It'll have to look just so."

"It's not a just-so house."

She exhaled a bit of air at me. Caro's out-breaths expressed an eloquent range of disapproval. An inch of time passed before I realized it was my turn to say something.

"Yes, I want to buy the place. No, I'm not going to sabotage a sale. Okay?"

"I didn't think you would. I was just—"

She shook her head: the impossibility of the house, or of the family, or of me. We both let it go with – at least on my side – a sense that we'd avoided a storm.

Caro let the agent in while I made gestures in the direction of work, and the woman ticked across the dining room in her heels so she could shake my hand and leave me her card. She'd attended some seminar where they told her to connect with the clients – all the clients, not only the ones you identify as the decision-makers. So business couldn't be done until she'd connected. I set her card beside the nearest mound of papers and she ticked back to the entryway with Caro, where they discussed the house's liabilities, not the least of which was the neighborhood.

"It is a Craftsman," she said. "That's a plus."

If she saw anything else for the plus column, I didn't hear about it. Caro might have miscalculated by getting a high-end agent for a low- to mid-range property. I figured the woman had only accepted because she owed someone a favor.

They carried their disappointment into the kitchen, discussed where to place Josie's woven basket, took their pictures once the feng shui was as perfect as they could manage in this imperfect setting.

"Can I interrupt for a minute?" The agent – I'd already evicted her name from my memory – gave me a smile brittle enough to shatter lipstick. "Could I ask you to move for a bit?"

I turned off the screen and watched from the doorway while she rolled my chair aside, worked out an angle that disappeared the desk, the computer, the papers. Caro had raised

the threat of painters again – no repairs, just cosmetic stuff –
but I'd vetoed them as too much of a disruption. Which they
would be, but the reason came after the refusal. We might
get more money if the place had a coat of paint, but that was
only a possibility. What was beyond doubt was that they'd
cost money I didn't have, and that Caro could overrun my
life without even noticing she'd done it.

I left them and reclaimed the kitchen, finding the dish
drainer they'd hidden under the sink and plonking it back
on the drain board, moving Josie's basket back to the table.

"The bedrooms are through here," Caro said. "Plus one
upstairs. Or two, really, but you have to go through one to get
to the other. It's cold up there. It's been shut off."

They clacked up the stairs and moved furniture across
the floor to inch it closer to the dream someone might be
chasing.

Everything is temporary, I told myself. Real estate agents
are temporary. Aunts are temporary. Even life is temporary.

When they left, I drove to the co-op. I might have broken up
with Shar and the Household, but I hadn't broken up with
the store where Shar worked. I needed a chunk of cheese,
they had better cheese than the supermarket, and I was going
to damn well keep shopping there.

I sat in the parking lot while the heat drained through the
car's metal, glass and plastic and dissipated into the winter
air. Then I pulled myself into Zanne stance – a plumb line
could have dropped straight down my spine – to walk in, but
it wasn't Shar I ran into, it was Zac. By the time I saw him, I'd

picked up a can of black beans, a bag of dried apricots and a glowingly beautiful head of red lettuce, and I hadn't taken a basket because I was only going to grab some cheese.

Zac was standing by the coffee grinder, pouring whole beans in at the top while the ground ones poured into his bag at the bottom. If you wanted a cartoon of simple living meeting the forerunners of gentrification, he was your model. He made the neighborhood look alternative and safe and partially white until the gentry gathered its money again, getting ready to come along and push him and everyone else out. Although you could use me as a model just as easily. I didn't wear my jeans until they were as close to the thread as Zac did, but by American standards I actively nonconsumed, and didn't I want to fresh-grind my coffee at the store exactly the way he did? Didn't I buy fair trade beans even though I knew the fairness went only as deep as the growers instead of filtering down to the people who worked for them? Hadn't I read that the big growers, with their unfair beans, were likely to pay their workers better? Sit down, Summer, and enjoy a nice cup of organic, fair trade, free-range coffee. The world's a terrible place and people suffer for your luxuries, but hey, you've made your gesture.

I stopped at the top of the aisle and watched Zac. I could've turned the other way if I'd wanted to. For that matter, I could've walked behind him and he wouldn't have noticed. He was focused on his coffee. But I called his name.

It wasn't loud enough to cut through the grinding, and I walked up to him and put a hand on his arm.

He glanced my way, said, "Hey," and, "Give me a minute here."

The beans ran through and the machine stopped, leaving silence behind. Or what seemed like silence after all that noise. He said, "I was hoping I'd run into you."

He dropped the bag a couple of times to settle the grounds, brushed the last bits off the spout and sealed the top before he turned to me.

"You're okay?"

"I'm good, yeah."

"Still at Josie's?"

"Still there."

We nodded a couple of times, filling the time till we figured out what came next. This was the problem with being in a relationship the culture didn't have a pattern for: It gave us no pattern for how to end it. When we started, it was all hormones and theories and momentum, and they helped us make the shape we wanted. But what were we to each other now? Friends? Exes? Former not-partners?

He said he'd been going to call and some part of me I hadn't known about straightened up and thought, *I matter to him*. And almost as quickly, the rest of me felt the Household's gravity and I pulled myself to a safer distance.

"I've been putting together this kind of introductory firearms class. Basic stuff. Maintenance, safety training, self-defense, a bit of target shooting, a bit of stuff about what the laws are, a bit of political awareness. You should join us."

The lettuce dripped onto my wrist and I shifted it.

"Not my thing, Zac."

"You don't know that. Firearms are fascinating. Really they are. And it's something we should all be doing. They're coming for us, Summer. They're coming for us all."

I said, "Zac." Not because I needed to call him out of a crowd or because I didn't have his attention but because it seemed like a way to tell him I meant this. "No one's coming for us."

"Not today they're not, but you can't have this many guns washing around the country, and this much anger, without something ugly happening. If it's not the government, it'll be some right-wing militia. Some neofascist group. We have to match them."

"And you're going to hold them off single-handed."

"Not single-handed. That's why you need to get involved. That's why we all do. We've got to prepare for this."

The lettuce was leaking onto my cuff. They sprayed water on the whole salad display. It kept everything looking fresh and lovely and buyable. It also made the lettuce rot faster, or so Shar had told me. Even the co-op had to play dirty if it wanted to sell us stuff, and if it wanted to stay open it did have to keep selling. I had an impulse to weep the tears I hadn't wept for Shar. For the lettuces of this world. For the underpaid people who pick the coffee beans and roast the coffee beans and heft massive damn sacks of coffee beans to get them from here to there and from there to somewhere else. For all the people who weren't armed and for all the ones who were. For Josie. For myself now I was without her. For Zac wanting to call me only so he could add me to his firearms class, because had we ever been friends really?

And for the struggle. The first time as tragedy, the second time as farce.

Zac was still talking at me. The history of armed self-defense. The Black Panthers. The Holocaust. What would've happened if the Jews had been armed?

"They'd have died differently, Zac, but believe me, they'd have died. They were a minority, and a small one. You have any idea what happened to the Panthers? To Fred Hampton? You know about the Warsaw Ghetto Uprising? You know what happened to Che in the mountains? The revolution doesn't just happen because you pick up the gun."

A man passed us with a toddler in the seat of his shopping cart, her pink snowsuit unzipped to the waist. With the instinct of conspirators, we stopped talking and turned our heads to watch them.

Zac hadn't quoted Mao about power growing from the barrel of a gun, but I supplied the words silently and asked myself what good a gun was in this age of drones and night vision goggles and heat-seeking fucking missiles. We'd be as underweaponed as the Spanish Republic had been. We might as well go into battle waving plastic light sabers.

I was – I still am – an encyclopedia of revolutions, of peaceful transitions, of failures. A specialist in some of history's most fascinating and depressing corners. But I don't know if my examples demonstrate that we can't win or only that we haven't yet. What I do know is that the need for a revolution doesn't go away.

It would've been easy enough for me to offer Zac an argument or three in favor of guns, but I didn't. Chile tried a peaceful transition to socialism, but the government it elected didn't have the backing of the army and didn't have armed civilian support, so it was overthrown. Violently.

Whenever we weren't preparing to fight, then, were we preparing to lose? What if a hundred Chilean Zacs had each trained a hundred people to use weapons, every year for decades? What were the odds that the coup would have played out differently?

And what if a hundred Zacs trained a hundred left-wing Americans to shoot and they all got as crazy as the right-wing Americans? What if every one of them lost sight of the goal?

"Wrong tactic, wrong time," I said.

"It's not because of you and Shar, is it? Because you don't have to break up with the Household just because you and Shar broke up."

I put a hand back on his arm. It was awkward, pressing groceries into my body, reaching out only from the elbow. I didn't say, "I can't live that way." I didn't say, "If it weren't for the Household and the guns, I'd still be with Shar." I squeezed his arm and let that mean whatever he wanted it to, and I left to pay for my black beans, my heartbreakingly pure lettuce, my dried apricots, my cheese.

In the car, all the anger I hadn't felt in the store landed on Zac for trying to hold onto me, and on myself for not telling him I was fully and permanently gone. On Shar for drawing me into a way of life I didn't want to live anymore, one I might never have wanted to live if every hormone my body produced hadn't been singing arias at the prospect of seeing what would happen if we touched *there* and I didn't put my clothes back on and run away.

I'd never broken up with a theory before. I hadn't left her because the sex had gone dry or because we were fighting about who was supposed to clean out the tub. It wasn't even about the guns, although they came into it. It was because I couldn't pretend anymore that sharing partners was a revolutionary act, or even a political one, and with that thought something nonmaterial but very real – the anger, probably, but sadness was mixed into it – quietly folded itself away. Whatever came next, the Household was past. Shar was past. I sat in my cold car with my breath frosting the windshield and felt something surprisingly like peace.

18

WHEN David finally called, it was with none of the hesitation I'd grown used to.

"This is all very last-minute, but I wonder if you'd join me for dinner tonight. I thought it might be nice to get together without an agenda."

That was an agenda – let's get together and not talk about the one thing you want to talk about – but when I'd asked him to support TOCK I'd given up the right to say that. I'd given him permission to ever so considerately take over my life.

"Can you live with someplace" – I searched for a neutral word – "less formal?"

He suggested Cobalt, which wasn't far enough down the scale for comfort, but it was an improvement: white light with flashes of blue neon replacing the honeyed yellow of old money.

He got there ahead of me, and again he stood and didn't offer to shake hands – he wasn't that sure of me – but his face lit up.

"What a pleasure," he said.

I said it was good to see him, and in an uncomfortable sort of way it was. I could have written a six-page essay on why I shouldn't like this man, and twelve on the conflicted ways I didn't, but even so, some unexpected butterfly inside me felt the sun's warmth and opened its wings to let them dry.

We filled a few minutes with how-are-you's and a few more by picking our way through the menu and discussing what we'd eat, with David urging me toward an appetizer, a drink, a salad, surely a dessert when the time came: more, grander, pricier.

He'd met Caro, he said after the waiter took our orders. She was an impressive woman. It was such a pleasure to have the family back in his life.

I made noncommittal sounds – enough to keep from sounding sulky but not enough to feel fully complicit. He was saying, "See what I can do now I'm here?"

By the time our salads came, he was talking about Josie. Our most reliable topic. As if during all those years without her, no one had been able to hear what he needed to say.

"It's odd, but I have a memory – one of those pictures the mind holds – of her wearing white dresses, although I can't believe the memory's accurate. For all I know, I remember one dress and I've multiplied it. It's an unlikely thing for her to wear, don't you think? Maybe that's why it stuck in my memory."

"What was she like back then?"

"Omniscient."

I laughed, although in some corner of my mortal soul I still believed she was.

"Of course, you have to remember the difference in our ages."

He went over old, fond territory: How much time she spent with him. The candy that mattered so much because it was forbidden at home. The places she took him. I didn't recognize much of the Josie I knew. She had none of the wryness, none of the strength. Maybe those come to a person later. Maybe he didn't know how to see them, at least in her.

"I remember our mother trying to teach her the piano. It was a source of real conflict between them, because Josie was determined not to learn and my mother took a long time to admit defeat. Or it seemed like a long time. Maybe the piano wasn't proletarian enough for her, although she wouldn't have known the word then. I never thought to ask. At that age, one takes a great many things as givens. She was hopeless at it, though, and I do think it was deliberate."

"I don't know. I don't think she had much of an ear. She used to sing to me, and she was always off-key."

I was smiling. I didn't explain why being off-key was such a gift, but in the way people do, he smiled back. Maybe it was only the fondness in my voice.

"Perhaps these things skip a generation," he said.

I asked if his mother had taught him as well. I heard myself say "as well". His formality was catching.

"Regrettably, no. I don't know if it was considered unsuitable for a boy or if her experience with Josie kept her from trying, but she never suggested it and it didn't occur to me to ask. Which is a pity, because she'd have been delighted, I think, and I'd have enjoyed it."

He sipped his wine – a thoughtful process, as if he was filtering it for tastes and overtones, comparing them to other wines he'd held on his tongue.

"That's not to say I would have had any talent, but I would have loved to try. I was hurt, in fact, that she didn't suggest it. I assumed she knew something about me that held her back."

He pulled into himself for a moment, then reconnected.

"What about you? Do you play an instrument? Do you sing?"

"I have an allergy."

"To?"

"Zanne. She's been offering to teach me guitar ever since I stopped wanting to learn it. Before that, she couldn't be bothered. It was, 'Here, I'll do the chords and you strum,' so it didn't sound awful, but I didn't learn anything."

"It sounds like a difficult childhood."

I hadn't told him that, so unless he thought not learning the guitar constituted trauma, Caro had been filling his ear with the family's failings.

"It would have been—"

I turned away, focused on a blue streak of neon on a lighter blue wall. What shade was cobalt anyway? A waiter passed, as crisp and efficient as all the waiters who eased David's passage through life. The words I couldn't say were *if Josie and Sol hadn't been there.*

"Sorry."

"Perhaps we should talk about something else."

Perhaps. No other living being said *perhaps.*

"That'd be good."

A waiter collected our salad plates, and by the time he left David had found a topic.

"Did Josie tell you much about Broadway Fashions?"

"Only that it existed."

That David was the son and heir, a phrase she said with a small, bitter laugh. Would she have been a Communist if being female hadn't excluded her from the succession? I liked to think so, but wondering was as pointless as asking how European history would have changed if the French Revolution had happened in Spain. She had been excluded, and being a girl was good training for being an American Communist. It taught her to notice the people who weren't allowed, who weren't given, who couldn't get. It taught her how to lose with dignity, how to live on small victories.

"As Josie used to talk about it, you'd have thought it was some huge corporation, but it wasn't. My father was a small businessman. A successful one, but nothing more than that. When I first came into the business, Broadway Fashions was a family business making inexpensive women's wear."

He talked about how first the Depression and then the war restricted women's ability to buy anything beautiful, so when the war ended the company was able to expand into an eager market. What he loved was the mix of style and business – not the money itself, but the joy of making it. He talked about how women's tailoring was different from men's, and the scope it gave to the imagination. He talked about color, pattern, texture. Our entrées came and his cooled on the plate while he talked about how cotton draped, how synthetics did, why the full skirt suited the human figure better than the straight. Not the female figure, the human one. I made myself set my fork down between bites as I listened, but by the time my plate was empty his was still two-thirds full.

"Are you still involved in the business?"

"This is the age of giants, and expansion is a young person's game, so in the end I sold and it was folded into something larger, which was folded into something larger than that. And of course everything's offshore these days. For a while you could still find the label, but even that's gone now."

How much had he sold it for, I wondered, and what happened to the people who'd worked for him? Had he moved production to Mexico before he got his money out? He cut a piece of fish and I cheered him on silently: *Eat more. Eat faster.* Instead, he raised it toward his mouth, then lowered it again, resting the fork on his plate.

"After the last time we spoke, I thought a great deal about the" – he paused here, searching for a word – "oddity of our conversation. You came to me about TOCK, and that's understandable. That's your job, and in addition you feel some – I suppose *attachment*'s the word – to the organization because of its connection to Josie. That was meant to set the limits of our discussion, and I'm afraid I broke that agreement when I asked what you yourself might want. But I do feel the need to take that part of the conversation further."

He paused again, like someone feeling his way in the dark.

"I'm not expressing myself very well. What I'm trying to say, and forgive me if I'm awkward, is that here was someone I care about, talking to me about money, which is always difficult, and I did ask, 'Is there anything I can do for you? Not for TOCK, for you?' but I'm not sure you really had a chance to answer."

He leaned toward me, and if he'd been offering me anything other than money – a book Josie bought him when he was a kid, a chocolate egg, his grandmother's hairbrush – I'd have said yes, we're family, I'd love to have it. Money, though—

Shit yes, I wanted money. I wanted it so I could tell Caro and her real estate agent to go fuck themselves. How much were we talking about anyway? House-price money? Down-payment money? Support-TOCK-myself money? Pay-back-the-student-loan money? Compared to Shar's, my loan was only the size of Delaware, but even so, I'd be paying it off till I was dead three times over.

Maybe we were talking about grocery-store money. Lots-of-candy money. Lots-of-strings-attached money. I-need-a-shower money.

Money never came free. From this man, I wasn't sure anything did. What I'd made was a physical decision, and maybe he read that in my body, because he pulled back toward his side of the table before I had time to say no.

One gift the Household had given me was that I knew how to live cheap. Not that I'd been a spender before, but I'd learned to make an art of it.

"There's nothing I need."

"I apologize. I think I crossed some boundary there. I only meant that I've been thinking about you, and I'd like to – be an uncle, I suppose."

The moment of real feeling had passed, though, fumbled by the offer of money, and what we had left was formality. We could have been diplomats, working out a treaty between nations. I said I'd like that, and he risked reaching a hand across the table. I squeezed it, he squeezed back, and for a short moment a current of emotion connected us.

Then we let go.

I still wanted money. I still needed that shower.

It was true that I never learned the guitar, but it wasn't true that Zanne only tried to teach me after I stopped wanting to learn. One time when I might have been ten – the guitar neck was wide in my hand but I was big enough to think I might manage it – we were sitting on my bed in the attic with the guitar in my lap. She placed my fingers on a C chord, and I'd watched hers often enough that it made an instinctive sort of sense. I could find the same places today and know I had it right. She showed me how to me push down on the strings until they cut grooves into my fingers, and then strum.

"It doesn't sound right."

"You don't have your calluses yet. You have to keep at it till you do."

I pressed harder and more painfully, but the sound stayed murky.

"Show me a real strum."

"That is a real strum. You strum your fingers over the strings, that's a strum. You're talking about picking."

Did I really not know the word or was I making a point of how far away from her I was? I don't know anymore. Too much time has passed. What I knew at the time was that I'd watched her right hand pluck notes out of the chords so the guitar sang the song on its own while her left hand hammered out another set of notes in a kind of commentary. That was what I wanted to do.

"You can't expect to sit down and play like a professional on your first try."

"I'm not some little kid who doesn't know what the guitar sounds like."

She laughed.

"You are some little kid."

I stood up and threw the guitar and the body hit the wall, jarring the strings into sound. Time froze while I waited to see if I'd smashed it. It was like pushing off a cliff with wings strapped to my back, not sure if I was going to glide or drop, not sure which would be more frightening. The possibility of hurting something Zanne loved was the rocky floor of the canyon below me.

Hurting Zanne was never a problem. Hurting something she loved though? That was new.

The sound died away and the guitar stayed whole. I said, "I hate you," with no thought about the damage that did, and I stomped down the stairs, leaving her on my bed.

For reasons I can't explain, I'm as ashamed of that memory as I am of anything else I can dredge from the sludge pit of my past. Far more than of the times I was horrible to Josie.

19

Rob knocked on the back door, saying he'd been at Irene's. He didn't ask if he could come in, but when I opened the door wide he stepped through and we hugged – sexlessly, almost formally. I found him a beer that had been in the refrigerator since I couldn't remember when, left by I had no idea who, and I made herb tea for myself, something golden that tasted of hay, from a box whose pictures promised deep sleep and jewel-colored dreams. I asked how it was going with Irene.

"She's a tough old bird. I like her."

"She does let you know where you stand."

"I think she'll see this through. I wasn't sure at first. Not everyone can."

I told him she didn't want anyone getting arrested over her house, then remembered he'd been there when she said it.

"Not everyone wants to go that route. But the other stuff – the paperwork, the lost sleep, the meetings with all those bastards who shake your hand and leave you feeling like you showed up in dirty pajamas. That can be just as hard. It grinds people down. It's meant to."

"I never thought of you as wearing pajamas."

"My mother was a big fan of pajamas. I had a pair with little footballs on them, and goalposts. I remember looking at them and thinking, 'These are weird.'"

"The pattern, or pajamas in general?"

"The pattern. I hated sports. They must've been on sale somewhere. I didn't know enough to question pajamas in general. I wouldn't have thought it was physically possible to get into bed without them."

He shrugged, shaking off the boy he'd once been.

"What Irene needs right now is support from the neighborhood, and the thing of it is, is she doesn't want to ask – it makes her feel like she's begging. Could you go around and talk to people with her?"

"What are we asking them to do?"

"Call the bank, write to it, ask it to sell the house back, taking into account what she's already paid for it. Turns out they did sell it, but they sold it to themselves and the sale was illegal. Not that it being illegal necessarily gets it back for her. Best thing is for people to send them a tweet – they hate that. It's public. She's working on a letter people can just sign and send, and we'll put out a request to our network, but it really helps to have the neighborhood behind her. If we've got enough people, she could host a get-together. How's she thought of in the neighborhood?"

"Depends who you're asking. When Shar and I were kids, her parents told us to stay away from Irene's boys. They were too tough for their daughter's delicate sensibilities. Too working-class, although they never would've put it that way."

Irene's kids had a basketball hoop over the garage where the neighborhood boys gathered, but never mind what Shar's parents wanted, I had my own reasons to stay away. The younger boy, the one closest to our age, talked about his father too much, too hard, too fast. His father was always about to take him hunting, or just had taken him hunting. They'd shot a deer, a moose, a bear. He never passed the limits of physical possibility – he didn't carry the bear out of the woods on his back or shoot a dinosaur – but I knew the hollow sound of a missing parent. He made my skin twitch as if a fly had landed on me.

"I didn't know you and Shar grew up together."

"Her parents sold up before I moved back in. They bought the house thinking the neighborhood was going to gentrify, and they lost the gamble. I never heard any other complaints about Irene. She doesn't deal drugs, she doesn't have parties that keep us up half the night, and she isn't, god forbid, a renter. Besides, even if someone doesn't particularly like her, they'd rather have her than an empty house."

I sipped my cup of cooling hay and told him about the neighbors I knew. He told me Irene would get me a copy of the letter so I could get my head around the details, although Irene would do the explaining. I was just there for support.

With that we ran out of business and we stared past each other for a bit.

"Shar tell you we broke up?" I asked.

He shook his head.

"I'm not exactly—"

He did a thing with his lips, as if he was sucking on a piece of candy.

"In on the secrets?"

"Part of the family. Same thing, I guess."

If I'd drawn a picture of the Household, I'd have lined us up like the people in a kid's drawing, all holding hands, with me on one end, Tee on the other and Shar and Zac in the middle, linking us. I was so conscious of being on one end that I never stopped to think about who we left out, with all our talk about love and openness.

"That kind of sucks."

"It's okay. I've been thinking it's time for me to go anyway."

"The air getting hard to breathe?"

"I like them well enough. It's all that business with the guns. I was talking to Zac about an occupation at one of the houses I'm working with – it didn't happen, but I thought it might – and he starts wanting to show up armed."

"The fuck."

"So I thought, *This might be the time to get out of here*."

I repeated "fuck," drawing it out so it was long and breathy.

"He wasn't going to shoot anyone, at least not on purpose. I don't think he's got that in him. He just – what he said was he'd keep it legal and safe but it was important to make the point."

"The hell, though."

"I told him, what's legal and safe if you're white and supporting the Second Amendment isn't the same as what's legal and safe if half a dozen of you are brown and occupying a house some bank claims to own."

We let that settle into a small silence while I tried to match it with the Zac I'd known. It sounded like Zac 2.0 – one of those upgrades you never meant to download.

"I've got space here," I said.

I listened to myself as if I was listening to a stranger. It was interesting, what I'd said. I did have space. Rob could move in. But I wondered how I felt about it.

Mostly, I thought, it would be good to have another human being in the house. He could take the upstairs. We'd only have to see each other in the kitchen, unless we wanted to. And this was Rob. It wasn't forever, just until it didn't work anymore or the house sold.

"As long as you're not storing surface-to-air missiles in the basement or anything."

"They'd rust down there."

"Damp?"

"Always."

We went through the business side of things – the place was going up for sale and I wasn't paying rent so for now, at least, why should he? – but we'd already made our agreement. We were like two people who shed half their clothes before they think to ask about syphilis, herpes, HIV.

He still had most of his beer, and a silence settled into the space between us. It was restful, having a low-drama human in the house. This was Rob the person, not Rob the organizer or Rob the Household's hobo roommate. He was a good person and, I thought, a lonely one. From the days when I still slept with men came the thought that if I'd been straight I might have made a move toward him. Not because I was attracted but because it was a channel for the current of feeling that ran between us to flow through. Or the current of feeling that I assumed ran between us. For all I knew, no one was in receiving mode on his end.

After a while we went back to talking about the neighbor-hood, house by occupant by hearsay by gossip, as if knowing everyone's stories would make a difference in who supported Irene and who didn't.

"I hate to say it, but I so don't want to go out door-knocking," I said.

"How come?"

"You know. Showing up on people's doorsteps. They're making lunch or the kids are crying or they're trying to get six loads of laundry done before they go back to work on Monday and there I am asking for their time, first to listen to us, then to send a letter to a bank? Normal people don't write to banks. I grew up with this whole set of beliefs that everybody else thought was either insane or danger-ous and that I was too young to defend, or even really to understand what I'd signed up for, so I learned to keep them to myself."

"No, I get that. What I was wondering was why you hated to say it."

"Josie was a lot to live up to. That's all."

I wasn't sure that answered the question he hadn't exactly asked, but he sipped his beer as if it had. I sipped cold tea and for no particular reason drifted into telling him how Josie and Sol met. I was comfortable enough, sitting with him, that when the thought wandered across my mind I followed it.

It was at the end of the war, I told him, during that kind of collective breath of relief when the threat of fas-cism was over and the Cold War hadn't fully set in. The soldiers came home, and Sol came with them. He'd been stationed in Alaska, counting caribou with the other politically undesirables.

Sometimes he told me he'd been counting potatoes. Or counting how many degrees the thermometer could drop below zero. Once he was sure I got the joke, he built on it. The reports he had to submit on the behavior of potatoes. How many carbon copies he had to make. The war wouldn't have been won without him. Those were the tales of heroism he'd wooed Josie with.

When he met her—

And he'd pause there.

The first time he did it, I thought he'd say she was the most beautiful woman he'd ever seen. I waited out the pause, and he held me with it the way Zanne would have, letting the beat carry on through the silence.

"She was the most real woman I'd ever known," he said instead, and I exhaled the way the whole country had at the end of the war. Forget beauty. Beauty had no value in our world. Josie was real, and Sol loved her for it.

"She didn't flirt. She didn't play games. If she said something, that was what she meant."

I didn't have Sol's gift for making a story live, and Rob was too flat to draw a performance out of me, so I told it in two dimensions, but it was still about Sol and Josie, and they were still in love.

"And then the Cold War started. The McCarthy era. I asked Josie once if they'd have had kids if they'd known what it would be like and she said, 'You have to. You can't let it stop you.'"

Rob sipped his beer. I touched my lips to my tea so he wouldn't be drinking alone.

He said they must've been scary times, but it came across as a match for my tea sipping, something to say so I wouldn't think I was talking alone.

"She always seemed" – I sifted through my memories for words that might make sense of her – "at peace with it. Maybe it was having the Party there for support. That sense they had that they were part of something larger, so even if the political situation was turning to shit where they lived, it was falling into place somewhere else."

"Even if in fact it wasn't."

"She didn't know that then. Neither of them did. Hell, maybe they were just tougher than we are. Or than I am anyway. I never had the sense the Red Scare hit them as hard as it would've hit me."

That thought rested between us while I wondered how much the work he did frightened him. The arrests. The charges his lawyer said would get bargained down to something more sensible.

"Do you think there'll be a revolution?" I asked.

Just a casual conversation between friends.

"I'll leave someone else to figure that out."

A pause.

"Any idea what replaces capitalism?"

"The Late Show?"

It was as good as any other answer as I'd gotten.

Some length of time later, he reached the end of his beer, and I showed him the upstairs rooms, found him a spare key, opened the heat vent. Then he went out the back door so he could cut through Irene's yard to his car. I watched him under the alley's streetlight, a small figure alone in the dark.

20

WHEN David Freund scheduled his visit to TOCK, he didn't go through me. He called Claudette and she called me. Did I want to be there?

Of course I wanted to be there, and I showed up easily a quarter of an hour before we were supposed to meet so Claudette and I could touch base.

What base was I hoping to touch? I had no idea, and I was only hiding behind the phrase because of how hazy I was. I knew I needed to fill her in on something, and I'd given it plenty of thought, but my mind kept darting away before it did anything useful with the question. Blame my discomfort with the man. My mixed feelings about him. How unsure I was about where we – Claudette and TOCK and my own particular self – stood with him.

I needed to switch metaphors and tell her the cards I held weren't promising. If we were lucky, she'd find a way to make use of them. If not, at least she wouldn't expect me to pull one out of my sleeve. When you're not sure what game you're playing, it's hard to slip the right ones up there. Did I want an ace? A joker? Had we gone back to baseball?

Only we didn't get a chance to talk, because David Freund was already with her when I walked in, settled into her office with a leather-covered notepad balanced on his well-pressed trouser leg. In his presence, the walls suddenly needed paint and the floor could have profitably reacquainted itself with a coat of wax.

He'd already made half a page of notes.

I couldn't remember any potential donor before him who'd made notes. Maybe they should, all of them, but it seemed to accuse me, although I wasn't sure what of.

Claudette interrupted herself enough to smile at me, to say hello, and David stood up to shake my hand, knowing I'd have to take it.

"We're just reviewing a few numbers," David said.

I nodded. Claudette could run him through enough numbers to sound organized, but she'd never been on friendly terms with them, and she used my interruption to detour into stories, where she was a master. The kids and their struggles took shape for David, and behind them, their parents, their schools, the entire underfunded, politically tormented school system. She pointed at a felt-tip drawing on the wall – a brown circle for a face, the glasses round and askew, the eyes behind them wide circles with a dot in the center of one and off to the side the other. In uneven lettering at the bottom, it said, "cladEt", the *E* squeezed in high above the *D* and the *T* because it got there late, the way I had.

"When Tyrone first came to us, he wouldn't even try to write."

He was nine and had been bumped from foster home to foster home until he landed in one that made time for him.

Good people, Claudette said. They'd brought kids to TOCK before. By the time the county moved him again, he was reading aloud and writing.

"We didn't get as far as spelling." She gave a small laugh, practiced but still real. "It's hard when you don't know how long you have with a kid, and spelling's not the priority. His next school will have a starting place. He knows he can make marks on the page and not be told off for it. It may sound small, but it's the difference between functional illiteracy and bad spelling."

And so on, the parade of small rescues. David nodded, but he'd stopped taking notes. It was numbers that moved him to spread ink across the page. I needed to remember that. He wasn't making any of those small, needling comments, though. Maybe he saved those for family – the descendants of Josephine Freund Dawidowitz.

Claudette moved on to the way TOCK worked with the schools, with the parents, the times it pushed the school board about one thing or another, the way it lobbied for better funding – the organizing that had been Josie's focus and that had taken a step back when Claudette moved into the leadership.

Eventually she stopped herself – there was no limit to the stories she could unroll – and asked if she'd given him a good enough picture of the organization.

"You've been more than generous with your time. I have a lot here to think about."

"We'll stay in touch, then."

They stood. I stood. We shook hands all over again to prove how well we all thought of each other. If it had been

up to me, I'd have pushed toward some sort of commitment – or I liked to think I would have – but I'd been
sidelined and whatever they were negotiating had slipped
away from me.

We walked him to the stairs, said another goodbye, and
turned back to Claudette's office, closing the door behind
ourselves.

"What time did he get here?" I asked.

"Maybe ten minutes before you did. Or twenty. I'd have
waited—"

She shook her head: it couldn't be done.

"How'd it go?"

"Hard to say. I know Josie's history with him, but really,
he couldn't have been nicer. He was—" She shook her head
again to say she was having trouble finding the right word. "A
gentleman. He was a real gentleman."

I laughed.

"He is that."

"You sounded like Josie for a minute there."

"I feel like I've been channeling her sometimes lately."

"You believe in that?"

"Not a chance."

"She wouldn't have either."

She crossed to the coffee pot in the corner and held it up,
her eyebrows making the gesture into a question, and she
pulled cookies from her desk drawer and passed me the box.

"I don't suppose he committed himself to anything,
did he?"

"I didn't want to push. It's early. Let's just have a pleasant
interaction, give him something good to take away."

I looked for a way to explain why it bothered me, David edging me out this way. It wasn't like I wanted to keep him to myself and it wasn't like I needed to claim credit with Claudette. All I knew was that it bothered me.

21

I GOT home to find the door unlocked and one of the newscasters on *All Things Considered* telling the empty kitchen what a sorry state the world was in. The unlocked door should have worried me. Rob and I were city people. We locked doors. But by the time I'd taken it in I was inside, and what burglar turned on Public Radio? Plus Josie's biggest pot was simmering on the stove, filling the kitchen with the smells of beef stock and my early childhood. From the living room came the sound of a guitar. I sighed – an action so involuntary I didn't know I'd done it until I heard myself.

"Sweetheart," Zanne called. "Come in. I made soup."

I stayed in the kitchen, leaving my jacket on as if I might still turn around and head back into the cold. My strategies for resisting Zanne were as instinctive as they were ineffective. I could see them for what they were and I was doomed to repeat them. Which I could also see.

She came into the kitchen smiling as warmly as if I hadn't refused to come to her, telling me what she'd put in the soup, how long it had been since she'd cooked for me (ages, but her idea of time was even less accurate than mine), how happy she was to do it now. Soup was the only thing Zanne cooked, and when I was little she made it for whoever we stayed with: Zanne Says Thanks Soup. I can call up pictures of Zanne sautéing the onion, celery and carrot, humming some song, noodling around in a minor key, opening drawers and cupboards, looking for a knife, a cooking spoon, the lid to a pot, the organizational principles of someone else's kitchen.

If our hosts were out when she started, she'd greet them with that same line, "I made soup," as if it was the greatest gift one human could bestow on another.

"I thought you'd left."

"I'm back. Take your coat off. I'll set the table."

I left my coat on, and instead of setting the table she took a bag of corn out of the freezer and poured some into the pot. When I was a kid, I chased the corn with my spoon, eating each kernel separately, popping the seed out before I chewed the rest. It must've taken me forever, although I don't remember anyone rushing me.

"How'd you get in?"

"With a key."

I didn't say, "You're not supposed to be here," but she heard it anyway.

"I grew up here too, you know."

"There was a rumor about that once."

I'd have to warn Rob about wandering mothers with keys. She hadn't been part of our non-negotiation.

She stirred the soup, ignored the sarcasm, set the table, moving around me as if it was perfectly normal to have a person playing statue in the middle of a smallish kitchen while she cooked.

When I was in my teens, Josie banned Zanne from the house if I was home.

"Summer lives here," she told Zanne on the phone while I listened through the floor vent in my bedroom. "If it's painful for her to see you, we have to respect that."

A long silence while Zanne made her case, or cried, or accused, or promised, or did all four.

"Don't be ridiculous," Josie said. "Of course I love you."

Only Josie could have linked "don't be ridiculous" and "I love you" without letting one cancel out the other. At the time, it seemed like a normal enough combination.

Standing in the kitchen, though, with my jacket hanging open, I could refuse to make Zanne welcome but I couldn't find the authority to keep her out. I watched her take soup spoons out of the drawer and set them on the table, then go back for knives, add butter, set out a loaf of French bread she must have bought on the way because it hadn't been in the house when I left.

When she started ladling soup into bowls, I jarred myself into motion enough to dump my jacket on the living room chair. Then we sat opposite each other and ate while she talked, trying topic after topic, looking for the one that would set off an echo in me. She was so happy to see me, she was staying with a friend in the suburbs, she hated suburbs, and did I remember our old apartment? It had the most beautiful woodwork.

In spite of myself, I said, "It did?"

"Dark wood. Stained, probably, but no one had painted it over and it gave the place a real sense of elegance. I loved that apartment."

Except for Zanne's scarf over the cardboard box, I didn't remember elegance. I remembered the stairway, the space heater with its terrifying flame, and two living room windows that looked out onto a tree and beyond that a parking lot. But Zanne saw what she wanted to and projected it like a slideshow.

"I've always been sorry it didn't work out for us to stay there."

I said nothing.

"I did try. I want you to know that. I couldn't make a living in one place."

I looked up from my soup and caught a glimpse of the Zanne who lived behind her familiar surface.

Don't feel sorry for her, I warned myself, but all the same I said, "I never knew that."

"I explained the whole thing. I never kept secrets from you."

"I was *five*, for chrissake."

"I can't help it that you were five."

"I'm not asking you to. I'm telling you: If you told me why we left, I didn't understand. Because I was five. So I never knew."

Somewhere at the back of my brain was the thought that this could reconcile us. She didn't abandon me because she got restless. She couldn't make a living in one place. But nothing inside me changed. No birds chirped out ballads about forgiveness.

"I should have reminded you. Maybe it would have helped."

"I doubt it."

I'd fallen into the flat voice I saved for Zanne: my you're-not-going-to-get-me-excited-about-this voice.

"Sweetheart," she said, and because she didn't follow it with anything – no plea, no decorative touches to make it more acceptable – I seemed to hear real grief in the word. If I'd let myself, I would've wept.

"Don't, Zanne. Please. Just don't."

"Don't what? Call you sweetheart? You are my sweetheart."

I rested my head in both hands. This was what happened between us. No matter what I said, no matter what I did, at some point my vision of reality went wavy and the next thing I knew I'd done her wrong again. She loved me. I was a coldhearted monster.

I gathered enough of myself to shake my head – leaning it into the right hand, leaning it into the left – in a kind of generalized no since I couldn't marshal any arguments or even say what I was arguing against, and I was saved from the conversation's downward spiral by Rob blowing in the back door, all parka and cold air. He rested a hand on my shoulder as he passed. I pressed his hand and introduced them: room-mate; Zanne. Explanation of the one, no explanation of the other. I could fill him in later.

"There's soup," I told him, pointing to the stove.

"Thanks."

He shed layers, filled a bowl, and although I invited him to sit with us – just the slightest bit desperately – he carried it upstairs. He had work, he said.

Zanne waited till the door at the base of the stairs closed before she started.

"Roommate?"

"Roommate."

"Just a roommate?"

"The fuck, Zanne. You think because I share the house with a man I have to jump into his bed? What is wrong with you?"

"I'd like a grandchild. That's how they happen. What's wrong with that?"

Before I had a chance to tell her how many things were wrong with it, someone knocked at the back door and I opened it to Irene. With that same edge of desperation, I invited her in.

"You're eating. I just wanted to ask you about the house. I'll come back another time."

I wasn't sure if she meant her house or Josie's, and I didn't care.

"We'd be grateful for the company. Please."

She came in but refused soup. Still, she sat with us and I introduced Zanne.

"The singer." As if she'd been touched by the gods. "Josie was so proud of you."

"She talked about me?"

"We used to listen to your recordings."

I left them there, the mirror and its entranced subject, while I took my jacket off the chair and hung it up. I didn't usually bother, but it filled a few seconds. Then I went to the bathroom to throw cold water on my face, hoping that when I lifted my head I'd feel like a new person, or at least like the old one but at the start of a new day. Nothing changed, though. I was me, and Zanne was still in my kitchen. The only difference was that I had a wet face.

After that, I couldn't think of anything to do but dry my face and go back.

I found them tipped toward each other across the table, as if the force of gravity had drawn them there. They could have been in love. In a sense, I suppose they were: Irene with Zanne's scrap of fame and Zanne with Irene's love. I made coffee and distributed it. I set out cookies. It wasn't as if Zanne would leave any sooner if I kept them in the cupboard. She had an audience.

And yes, I did notice how petty I was but it didn't strike me as something I could change. Or necessarily wanted to.

Zanne was listing the records Josie and Sol had owned when she was a kid. She must've hoped an interviewer would ask about her influences one day, and since none had Irene would work as a stand-in, although the artists wouldn't have meant anything to her. Irene knew Elvis and the Beach Boys, not Pete Seeger and Odetta. Her voice was doing that trick it did sometimes – the one she'd been trying on me when we first sat down. Whatever she was saying, it was the most intensely personal thing anyone had trusted you with, ever. Even if a minute later you forgot what she'd said, you still felt the pull of that voice.

"They let me put them on the record player myself when I was" – she held a hand about waist-height from the floor – "maybe so high. And that let me find my own way into the music, decide what I liked, how often I wanted to hear something. It let me make it my own somehow."

Irene nodded, nodded some more – *I'm an empty vessel; keep pouring* – and Zanne poured out the names of more singers she'd loved, their songs, their records, the scratch

Caro put in one of her favorites because she was jealous, although she swore to this day it had been an accident and Josie had believed her. Josie and Sol always took her side. Because of all the kids she was the least like them and they felt guilty about that. Zanne never understood what they had to feel guilty about but feel it they did, and Caro knew it. She had a gift for sensing weakness, and for using it.

"There's no point in guilt," she said. "It never did anyone any good."

If she'd felt some, it would have done me all kinds of good. I was sure of that.

I licked a fingertip and pressed it onto the cookie crumbs on my plate so I could lick them off. I sipped my coffee while it was still too hot, partly because it kept me busy and partly because Zanne had said it was bad for me. The day Zanne tells me not to do something and I don't rush out and do it, I'll know I've gotten over her having left me. In the meantime, I was enjoying myself, in a miserable sort of way.

Zanne talked about performing, about how much being on the road took out of her, sounding as if she wanted nothing more than to find herself a house with a white picket fence, throw her suitcases away and spend her time baking bread, although her face glowed with the pleasure of her complaints. That cold, open field.

As a kid, I thought I had to choose between the two versions of life the song offered, and the open field wasn't just the moral choice, it was the only possible one. By now, though, I'd grown a crop of doubts. I might not be sure what a goose-feather bed was, but it sounded warm, and since I didn't have a stifling husband expecting to share it, why not tuck myself in and have a good night's sleep?

Zanne nodded at me.

"She was a good traveler, this one. She slept backstage like an angel."

They turned to me, waiting for me to say my childhood sparkled with joy and stick-on glitter.

"Of course I slept. You put fuckin' brandy in my milk."

I'd never said this to her before. I'd barely said it to myself. It was a hunch, a jump my mind had made. For all that I don't like alcohol, I caught a whiff of somebody's brandy once and the scent unfurled in the top of my throat like a memory – the taste of those nights with my sippy cup and Zanne's voice threading its way into my sleep. I'd been fuckin' plastered.

She cocked her head to the side.

"What makes you say that?"

"It's true, isn't it?"

"Honestly, I don't remember how I got you to sleep. It just happened."

My lips did that Josie thing, the corners pulling back, the lips tightening.

"Don't give me that look. If I did – and I said *if* – it was because I had to. I wasn't some rock star, traveling with a nanny and a personal assistant and two different chefs, one to cook if I was hungry and the other one for if I wasn't. It was just me and you and the band. I did what I had to. To keep you with me."

I let the look stay where it was.

"Fine. Your mother was a monster. She probably gave you heroin too."

I got up, walked the circuit of the kitchen without finding anything to occupy me, and sat back down.

"Irene, I'm sorry. We do this. We can't sit together for ten minutes without doing it. I didn't mean to drag you into it."

"Hey, it's okay."

"It's not okay. It's horrible."

By way of killing the topic, I carried my plate to the sink.

"Rob talked to me about the letter," I said, edging Zanne out of the conversation. "About going with you when you talk to people."

"That Rob? He's a miracle."

"When do you want to go?"

After Irene left, Zanne nibbled a cookie and looked like she planned on spending the night.

"I was going to email you," I said, slotting myself back into my place at the table, "but as long as you're here I won't. I want to buy the house from the three of you, contract for deed. Caro hasn't agreed yet – she thinks it'll sell and she'll have an avalanche of money, so we haven't worked out the details, but in principle are you okay with that?"

"Why wouldn't I be?"

"You wouldn't get the money up front. On the other hand, you'd have some coming in every month."

She studied me, which involved doing that Zanne-ish tip with her head and staring meaningfully. Lovingly. Somethingfully. I held her gaze, trying not to think she owed me this, which is another way of saying that's exactly what I thought.

"You know what happens to me and money," she said after what seemed like a long time but couldn't have been. "A bit every month might be better than an avalanche."

I did what I could to look happy but it wasn't a good fit. My mind was assembling the list of numbers I'd need for Caro: a price lower than the real estate agent's but not so low that it closed off the discussion. An interest rate. This past year's income, and by way of comparison, the year before's. How much it would've cost if we'd paid someone else for the job I did. The cold stone of calculations and from that ground the leap into full guilt trip.

Did Summer need anything?

You're god damn right she did. She needed to stop hiding behind herself.

I thanked Zanne. The words were a few beats too late, but they'd made a solemn procession through my mouth and into the air.

2 2

M ORE than a week after David graced TOCK with his presence, Claudette called me.

"David Freund," she said, pausing to paint it a light shade of irony onto his name, "has made a pledge. That was the good news. The rest of the news is that he wants to be on the board."

I was still stuck on the good news, thinking it should've made me happy and knowing it felt like a punch in the stomach. He'd left me out of the conversation. I couldn't have said why I cared, but I did. I felt – what? Hurt that Uncle Summer-Matters-So-Much-to-Me was pushing me aside?

Maybe.

Did I want to matter to him? Not exactly. He still kind of made my skin crawl.

But.

But, but, but.

Maybe I wanted to be the one to edge him out. I didn't know. All I was sure of was that I didn't like it.

"How much?" I asked.

"He hasn't given me a number. Roughly what he was giving Josie."

"And I don't suppose he'll say how roughly until he's on the board, will he?"

"You know him better than I do. You think it'll be much less?"

"Are you kidding? I don't know him well enough to have predicted he'd edge me out. I do know he likes to mess with people. That's all I can tell you for sure."

"He'll be all kinds of fun then, won't he?"

"What did you tell him about the board?"

"I told him it wasn't my decision, and it's not."

We let a bit of silence slip through the wires connecting us. The board wasn't bad, as boards went. A couple of parents, some retired teachers, a couple of people with money and good intentions, one guy whose confidence outran his competence. I couldn't predict how they'd cope with David Freund.

"Have you told anyone yet?"

"I'm waiting for my head to stop spinning. But for that kind of money – however much that kind of money turns out to be – I don't see how they'll say no."

I nodded as if I thought she could see me. I was pacing the house, phone to my ear. Kitchen, dining room, living room, front door, living room.

"What do you think he wants to do there?" she asked.

"Honestly? I have no idea. Maybe nothing. Maybe it's just vanity. Or getting the last word in with Josie."

"We can hope."

"We might as well."

"In the meantime, I think I'll go ahead and shoot myself, if you don't mind."

"You got an extra bullet? I might want one."

"I'll bring it over as soon as I've used mine."

I should have laughed but didn't. The thought was too distant to turn into sound. We ended the call as unhappy as if our main donor had said he'd set his money on fire in a cold, open field before he'd give it to us.

23

O N the day Irene's house was repossessed, the weather enfolded us like a blessing from all the gods I don't believe in. The day lilies that had grown along her fence for as long as I remembered bloomed lemon yellow, and we carried her whole life past them with as little ceremony as if she'd be there to admire them tomorrow.

Her sons had turned out to help, along with their wives and a couple of men she introduced to me and Rob without explaining who they were to her. Family, presumably. Their names slipped away almost as soon as I heard them and I was too embarrassed to ask. Tommy, Johnny, Timmy. Derek, unless it was Darren. Hefty guys who knew how to steer an armchair through a door and queen-size box springs around the bend in the stairs. Rob and I carried the lighter bits of furniture, the boxes, anything too small for them to bother with, while the sons' wives packed the last stray bits from the kitchen cupboards and scolded the kids out of the way.

Irene stood at the back of the truck and gave orders. "Slide that along the wall. Look out for that, it's breakable. That's why it says fragile."

Pride told me to carry more, carry bigger, carry heavier, but the guys were twice my size and I was already lifting more than the other women and not much less than Rob. I organized him to take one end of the kitchen table while I took the other – lightweight stuff for the lightweights, but at least it was a two-person load. We tipped it on its side to maneuver it through the door, bumping a doorframe on the way out.

What the hell, it wasn't Irene's doorframe anymore. As long as the table was okay, it didn't matter.

Behind us, the kitchen stood gap-toothed, with blanks where the stove and refrigerator had been. She'd sold them. She'd given them away. For all I knew, she'd hauled them to the Mississippi and chucked them in. When you rent, you don't bring your own. When you get repossessed, you don't leave gifts for the bank.

We left the house unswept and empty, and Rob and I followed the truck to an apartment building near the post office. In the hall, scrapes marked the path where other people had carried their lives in and then out again. Irene stood by the apartment door and pointed: bedroom for that; kitchen; not sure, just dump it by the window.

It took a quarter of an hour and all four of the big guys to get the couch past the bend in the stairs, and they left a new scrape to say Irene had been there, even if she didn't want to be.

"You going to be all right here?" one of her sons asked.

"You think the boogeyman's going to get me?"

He looked around.

"Dunno. You think he might?"

The other son left to return the truck, the wives rounded up the kids and went home, and Rob opened boxes in the kitchen, handing me cooking oil, mugs, spaghetti, cans and jars and bottles as if I'd know what to do with them, but I had no better idea than he did and set them on the counter.

"Irene, you want me to put this stuff on the shelves? 'Cause I'm running out of space here."

"Put it anywhere. I don't like where it is, I'll move it."

I made choices: This goes on the shelf by the oven, that goes by the sink, and this other thing? It stays on the counter because I haven't found enough things like it to know how much space it needs.

It felt useful. It felt invasive. It felt like her life would go on.

Rob cut the bottom of an empty box and folded it flat on the narrow stretch of floor below the cabinets. Forget about a kitchen table here. A patch of linoleum sketched a dining room into the end of what was otherwise the living room.

One of the men whose names I'd lost came back with pizza and a case of beer, and we left the kitchen half unpacked and sat on the floor, wedged into the spaces between full boxes, and on randomly deposited furniture, passing food and beer. The guys teased each other but with Irene they were as gentle as if she'd shatter.

Empties collected on the floor. Irene lit a cigarette and carved ashes off into the neck of a bottle, working a skillful circle around the ember. She lifted her beer and held it up in Rob's direction.

"This guy. This guy may not've got me my house back, but he came through for me when no one else could. He's a fuckin' hero."

The guys roared and drank. I cheered. It wasn't the revolution. It was beer and pizza in an apartment where Irene smoked indoors. It was the smallest ember of a victory wrapped in layers of defeat.

It was what we had. It would have to be enough.

Josie Freund Dawidowitz

1955

O N the far end of the couch, Sol was snoring gently through the ads. He liked to call this one The Dancing Laxatives, and since he was missing it Josie thought the joke for him. For a flickering moment, it lifted the gloom the day had dropped on her, a damp, musty towel of a mood that had started when she told a mother she could challenge her daughter's school about placing the girl in a slow class.

The woman drew back as if Josie had sprayed spit on her.

If the school thought she was making trouble, the woman said, they'd take it out on her daughter. And besides, the slow class might give her a chance to stand out.

Oh, it might. And pixies might bring the girl a college degree in the darkest hours of night.

If the mother had been some fragile wisp of a woman, it wouldn't have bothered Josie much, but she was tough enough to leave Josie as flat as roadkill in the middle of TOCK's office. She'd brought her daughter to TOCK for help with her homework, the woman said, and that was all she was there to talk about.

Then, walking home from the bus stop, Josie had passed the old man who lived on the corner, and by way of saying hello he complained about the new bus schedules. He had to transfer twice to visit his son, and with each transfer he waited twenty minutes, half an hour.

"They're writing us off," he said. "If we don't drive, we're not rich enough to matter."

And against what she recognized as her better judgment, she said, "We could do something about that, you know."

He gave her a pitying half laugh and a narrow shake of his head.

"Can't fight City Hall."

The words summed up everything the roadkill mother had been telling her. You can fight the people who are trying to help you and you can fight your friends, but nope, you absolutely can't fight City Hall.

On a different day, she might've said, "The hell you can't." She might've said, "Oh, but I have." She might've said all kinds of things, only she didn't, she just blew an exasperated sigh into the air, leaving him to think he'd educated her about the world.

Come winter, you can stand at the bus stop till your lungs freeze, she thought at him now, then drew her mouth tight against herself. No one ever won an argument after it was over. She'd have to let this one go.

She called Sol's name, gently the first time, then again, louder. He was a dedicated sleeper, her Sol.

"It'll be on in a minute," she told him.

He snorted himself awake and was upright when the news started, fully conscious in time to watch Montgomery's sidewalks fill with a quietly unstoppable flow of Negroes. She wondered how far they'd walked that morning before starting work, and how early they'd gotten up so they could do that. How late it would be before their tired feet brought them home.

A near-empty bus rolled past, one white passenger visible through the open window.

As a piece of organizing, the boycott was inspired. No one could keep Montgomery's Negroes from walking or force them to ride a segregated bus if they chose not to. Not the mayor, not the police, not the Klan.

The hell you can't fight City Hall.

The Russian Revolution, she thought, must've had some moment like this, when a spark landed on a pile of straw and no one noticed until the whole place was in flames. The Paris Commune would've had some moment. The Spanish Republic, the medieval peasants' revolts, the wave of union-organizing that swept the US during the Depression. The spark never caught where you thought it would, or when, but over and over again people reached their limit and before anyone understood what was happening, the fires were burning.

Her eyes filled with unexpected tears and she thought about hiding them from Sol but let them spill over instead. They were an odd way to honor the moment she was witnessing, but that's what they seemed to be doing. She would've loved to be in Montgomery, organizing rides, raising money, making phone calls, doing whatever it was a northern white woman could do. She wanted to breathe the charged air of this quiet battle.

And when you're too far away to be of use? At the very least you can sit on your couch and weep.

A reporter interviewed someone, the news anchor came back on and said Josie had no idea what. Her mind had left them behind, revisiting instead the hope that had surged through her during the war, when the Soviet Union had been America's ally, when the country was going to come out of all that bloodshed fairer, better, more equal. With liberty and justice for all. With jobs, with education, with housing. With a chance – at the very least a chance – for every child. And above all with a population willing to fight City Hall, the school, the boss and three grizzly bears for what it needed.

Then the surge was gone, or its memory was, leaving her hollow and wondering what she'd accomplished in the last few years. Yes, she'd helped found TOCK, but what fires had TOCK sparked? Her days were swallowed up by walking kids through the multiplication tables, the alphabet, whatever it was they'd gotten lost in, then by coming home, feeding her own kids, breaking up their arguments, helping with their homework, going to meetings, coming home again, looking for a way TOCK could make more of a difference than it did and not finding it. TOCK's meetings turned passionate over the best place to buy pencils, and Party meetings—

She didn't like to put words to the question, but what difference did Party meetings make? Yes, they kept the members involved and the structure in place for a time when history's winds would swing around to blow from some new direction. But the meetings themselves? People talked about what they were doing in other organizations, and even though the organizations mattered, the discussions didn't. They were underlining in a book no one was paying attention to.

The thought that she could resign crashed like a rock though her mind's front window, leaving her too surprised to do anything more than notice its rockness, the sudden way it had gotten itself in. Then she made herself look at it. It hadn't landed there because she disagreed with the Party, but because everything it did seemed so pointless and sad. A political disagreement would at least show her some new direction. Without that, though, quitting would give her nothing but a few spare hours a month for life to stretch out in, bleak and meaningless.

Sol shifted down the couch and ran a thumb under her eye, not so much wiping away her tears as acknowledging them.

"They're magnificent, aren't they?" he said, nodding toward the people who were on the screen again.

They were, and she leaned into his solid shoulder, his warmth. Right there on their television, the Negroes of Montgomery, Alabama, were walking the long miles to work instead of sitting at the back of the bus, and they were unstoppable.

If they could do that, if no one could know what spark would ignite a bit of straw or what straw would ignite the prairie, then what right did she have to lose hope?